A Box of Matches

Nicholson Baker was born in 1957. He is the author of five acclaimed and extraordinary novels – *The Mezzanine, Room Temperature, Vox, The Fermata* and *The Everlasting Story of Nory* – and various collections of essays, including *The Size of Thoughts* and *Double Fold* for which the *New York Times* called him 'the Erin Brockovich of the library world'. He lives in Maine with his wife and two children.

ALSO BY NICHOLSON BAKER

Nicholson Baker

A BOX OF MATCHES

VINTAGE

Published by Vintage 2004

2 4 6 8 10 9 7 5 3 1

Copyright © Nicholson Baker 2003

First published in Great Britain in 2003 by
Chatto & Windus

Vintage
Random House, 20 Vauxhall Bridge Road,
London SW1V 2SA

Random House Australia (Pty) Limited
20 Alfred Street, Milsons Point, Sydney
New South Wales 2061, Australia

Random House New Zealand Limited
18 Poland Road, Glenfield,
Auckland 10, New Zealand

Random House (Pty) Limited
Endulini, 5A Jubilee Road, Parktown 2193,
South Africa

The Random House Group Limited Reg. No. 954009
www.randomhouse.co.uk

A CIP catalogue record for this book
is available from the British Library

ISBN 0 09 944838 6

Papers used by Random House are natural, recyclable products made from wood grown in sustainable forests. The manufacturing processes conform to the environmental regulations of the country of origin

Printed and bound in Great Britain by
Bookmarque Ltd, Croydon, Surrey

For Margaret

A Box of
Matches

Good morning, it's January and it's 4:17 a.m., and I'm going to sit here in the dark. I'm in the living room in my blue bathrobe, with an armchair pulled up to the fireplace. There isn't much in the way of open flame at the moment because the underlayer of balled-up newspaper and paper-towel tubes has burned down and the wood hasn't fully caught yet. So what I'm looking at is an orangey ember-cavern that resembles a monster's sloppy mouth, filled with half-chewed, glowing bits of fire-meat. When it's very dark like this you lose your sense of scale. Sometimes I think I'm steering a space-plane into a gigantic fissure in a dark and remote planet. The planet's crust is beginning to break up, allowing an underground sea of lava to ooze out. Continents are tipping and foundering like melting icebergs, and I must fly in on my highly maneuverable rocket and save the colonists who are trapped there.

Last night my sleep was threatened by a toe-hole in my sock. I had known of the hole when I put the sock on in the morning—it was a white tube sock—but a hole seldom bothers me during the daytime. I can and do wear socks all day that have a monstrous rear-tear through which the entire heel projects like a dinner roll. But at night the edges of the hole come alive. I was reading my book of Robert Service poems last night around nine-thirty, when the hole's edge began tickling and pestering the skin of the two toes that projected through. I tried to retract the toes and use them to catch some of the edge of the sock's fabric, pulling it over the opening like a too-small blanket that has slid off the bed, but that didn't work—it seldom does. I knew that later on, after midnight, I would wake up and feel the coolness of the sheet on those two exposed toes, which would trouble me, even though that same coolness wouldn't trouble me if the entire foot was exposed. I would become wakeful as a result of the toe-hole, and I didn't want that, because I was starting a new regime of getting up at four in the morning.

Fortunately last night I had an alternative. I'd brought a clean white tube sock to bed with me to use as a mask over my eyes, in case Claire was going to read late. I have to have darkness to go to sleep. I have one of my grandfather's eye masks, made of thick black silk probably in the thirties, but it smells like my grandfather, or at least it smells like the inside of his bedside table. The good thing about draping a sock over your eyes is that it is temporary. The sock slips off your head when you move, but by then you've gone to sleep and it has served its purpose.

So when the hole in the sock on my foot became intolerable, I reached down and pulled it off in a clean, strong motion and flipped it across the room in the direction of the trash can—although I have to say there is something almost painfully incongruous in the sight of an article of underclothing that one has worn and warmed with one's own body for many days and years, lying bunched in the trash. And then onto my naked foot I pulled the fresh sock that I'd had on my face. It felt so good: oh, man, it felt good, really good. I moved my newly sheathed foot back into the far region of the sheets and pulled the heavy blankets around me and I took my hand and curved it and draped it over my eyes where the sock had been, the way a cat does with its paw. Eventually Claire got into bed. I heard her bedside light click on and I heard the pages of her book shuffle, and then she twisted around so we could kiss good-night. "You've got your hand over your eyes," she said. I murmured. Then she turned and shifted her warmly pajamaed bottom towards me and I steered through the night with my hand on her hip, and the next thing I knew it was four a.m. and time to get up and make a fire.

2

Good morning, it's 3:57 a.m. and I'm chewing an apple. My name is Emmett, I'm forty-four, and I earn a living editing medical textbooks. I have a wife, Claire, and two children. When I made the fire in here yesterday, I clicked on a table lamp in order to see what I was doing. That was a mistake. You have to make the fire in the dark: it must become its own source of light. In fact you have to do as much in the dark as possible, including prepare the coffee, because when you turn on a light, your limbic system is hauled into the waking world, and you don't want that.

So this morning I made the fire by feel. There was no moon, or else it was obscured by cloud, so I couldn't even see where the fireplace was: it was just an empty hole of cold in the blackness. I bunched four balls of newspaper, and ripped up some of a pizza box and laid the ripped strips on them, and put some dried apple branches on top of that and some bigger logs higher up—really it's like building a sandwich, except that the lettuce is at the bottom. I pulled off a match from the matchbook that was there where it should have been on the ashcan, feeling the negative thump when the cardboard fibers tore away, and I was on the verge of striking it, when I decided to wait. I wanted to see the fire catch and confirm itself, but I wanted to watch it while sipping my coffee. So I put the match down next to the matchbook and felt my way towards the kitchen. There was a very faint green circle of light on the floor of the dining room that I thought was a diverted reflection of a distant streetlight, but it turned out to be coming from the tiny green bulb in the smoke detector in the ceiling.

I opened the cabinet and felt for a curve of mug. I didn't pull it from the shelf right away, since we sometimes pile mugs on top of mugs, tipping them slightly so that the top mug can rest there, and if I pulled a mug down without being careful, one of the upper-berth mugs might fall. But my octopuslike fingers found nothing nearby that was unstable, and so I took the mug down from the shelf. Which mug was it? I had no idea what color it was. I could feel the baked-on pattern under my fingers, but I couldn't make out what it was. We have several mugs from railroad museums; I thought it might be one of them.

The sink was a pale shape, above which, presumably, were the taps and the faucet: I positioned the mug where I thought it would be under the faucet and filled it with some water and drank. You should always start your day with a drink of water. Then I made coffee, also by feel, and there was a sudden howl of light when I opened the refrigerator to pour some milk in my coffee; and then I came back in here and put the coffee down on the top of the ashcan. It was time to light the fire.

I felt for the single match that I'd laid out in readiness. It wasn't there. I must have brushed it off when I was setting down the mug. No problem—I found the book of matches easily and opened it. Ah, but then my fingers felt nothing but cardboard stumps, like a row of children's teeth just coming in. It had been the last match in the matchbook.

Well, I needed a match to start the fire. I went back

into the dining room. Usually on the dining-room mantel
there is a little Japanese bowl with a matchbook or two in
it, because we have a fire in there when we have people
over for dinner. I started at the right-hand side of the
mantel and I made little finger-bunching motions—
match-bowl, match-bowl? I came to a small glass object
holding a squat low candle in it. The wick, because the
candle had been used, was very straight and hard and the
end of it crumbled a little when my finger touched it.
A little ways farther down was a bowl that I thought was
the one, but inside there were some dried things that
must be rose petals—it felt like a bowl of Special K. I
knew I'd gone too far down the mantel, so I worked my
way back, proceeding carefully in case there was some
trinket that I would make fall. I came to a semi-vertical
curving shape and remembered that there was an old
plate leaning there. I couldn't visualize the pattern of this
plate. Claire loves china but I can only keep in mind the
china we use every day.

No, there were no matches that I could find on the
dining-room mantel, and that meant I had to go back to
the kitchen to see if there were any matches on the back
of the stove. I should have thought of that right away. I

groped delicately along the surface above the oven dials, past the cool facets of the salt and pepper shakers, and finally I came to a shape that moved easily when I touched it: the red box of wooden matches standing on its side.

I walked back to the living room and took a seat in the fire chair, and I pushed open the drawer of the matchbox, feeling both sides of the inner sliding tray when it emerged to be sure that I wouldn't open it upside down and allow the matches to tumble plinkingly out, and I singled out one match and rolled its square shank between my fingers. When I struck it in the profundity of the dark I could see the dandelion head of little sparks shooting out from the match head and the eagerly waving arms of the new flame before it calmed down. The match flares more on the side away from where you slide it. Or am I wrong—is there more flare on the side that has touched the striking surface? I held the little flame to the scalloped hems of the balled-up newspaper lumps all along the front, and the fire worked its way in under the three logs, and soon I could feel its warmth on my shins.

3

Good morning, it's 4:45 a.m., and today after I made the fire I just sat for ten minutes doing nothing. Every so often I yawned, leaning forward in my chair with my elbows on my knees and my hands clasped. Sometimes a yawn will take on a life of its own, becoming larger and more extensive than I could have foretold, forcing me to bow my head and gape until several drops of saliva, fed by streams on the insides of my cheeks, collect at the corners of my mouth and fall to the floor. After a few large down-yawns like these, my eyes are lubricated and I can think more clearly. I don't know whether scientific studies of the human yawn have taken into account the way it helps to lubricate the eyeballs.

I do worry about the duck in the cold. She's probably

awake. We have a duck that lives in a doghouse outside. At night we drape a blanket over the doghouse and put a portable window screen over its front entrance. The screen is there to keep out foxes and coyotes. There is a red fox that lives on the hill with a bushy horizontal tail that is almost as big as he is, and at night sometimes you can hear the coyotes hooting from the fields on the other side of the river.

The duck's blue dish freezes overnight. Every morning, before I leave for work (dropping Phoebe at school on the way), I hit the bowl upside down against a snow-pile and a disk of ice plops out: the bowl is self-cleaning in this weather. There are several other ice disks lying around in the snow, and these are pecked at by crows in the daytime. They look like UFOs, or maybe more like corneas—the layer of half-dissolved duck food frozen at the upturned bottom is the iris. The duck emerges, making her tiny rapid cheeps, excited over the prospect of the warm water, which steams when I pour it in the bowl. She makes long scoops of water with her under-beak and then straightens her neck to let the warmth slide down. I hold out a handful of feed, and she goes at it with her beak, very fast, with much faster movements than humans can make, moving like the typing ball on an old IBM Selectric. Some of the feed falls in the water, and that gets her crazy: she roots around in the swampy warmth, rapping at the bottom and finding all the nuggets that swirl there, making the water cloudy with the outflow from her throat. After a last burst of eating she looks up and is still, working her neck twice to settle her breakfast, and she walks out with me down the driveway. Sometimes here she will flap her wings hard, high-stepping in place without becoming airborne, like a jogger at a stoplight; sometimes she takes flight, although she hasn't completely refined her landings. Her eyes are on the sides of her head: she has to turn away from me to look up at me, then out at the world, then up at me again.

Last night I was lying in bed when I heard a terribly sad sound, as of a cat in distress or an infant keening in the cold: long, slow, heart-rending cries. I half rose and held my breath and listened intently—was it the duck?—but the sound had stopped. I almost woke Claire to ask her what I should do. And then, as I resumed breathing, I realized that I was hearing a whistling coming from some minor obstruction in my own nose as I breathed.

At times, when I sit here, a long series of daytime thoughts will pass through me—thoughts connected with work or, say, with town politics. That's all right—let those thoughts pass through you. You hear them coming, like a freight train with the whistle and the dinging; they take several minutes to go by, and then they're gone. Remember that it's very early in the morning—early, early, early, early. Sometimes the stars are thrillingly sharp when I first get up and stand at the window on the landing of the stairs: private needle-holes of exactitude in the stygian diorama. Orion's belt is the only constellation that I recognize easily. The apportioning of stars into constellations is unnecessary: their anonymity enhances the sense of infinitude. This morning I saw a long pale mark like a scar across the heavens. It was the trail of a high jet, a night flight from somewhere to somewhere, lit from the underside by the setting moon. "A moonlit contrail," I whispered to myself, and then I came downstairs and felt for the coffeemaker.

4

Good morning, it's 4:52 a.m., and I'm very glad to be conscious when nobody else is conscious. To get to this point, where I am the sole node of wakefulness at the heart of the sleeping world, takes a fair amount of preparatory work. I have to get out of bed carefully, so as not to wake Claire, and I have to put on my bathrobe; I have to cinch snug the flannel sash and come downstairs by the front stairs, so as not to wake my son, whose bedroom is at the top of the back stairs, and I have to make coffee.

Making coffee in the dark, especially when the moon has set, or when there is no moon, is a skill that improves with practice. First you pull out the old filter, with its layer of coffee sludge, and pin its sides together like a soft taco so that you can get it safely into the garbage can without spilling, and then you rinse out the filter basket and the carafe, taking special care to clean the little hole in the plastic top of the carafe, which is like the hole in the top of a baby's head, where the coffee tinkles down from the basket and into the baby's brain. And you stretch the fluted mass of paper filters so that your fingers can feel and take hold of one layer—a sensation similar to turning the pages of an eighteenth-century book—and you settle the filter in the basket so that none of its sides are likely to flop over, allowing the water to flow around the coffee without drawing out its liquor. When in darkness you scoop new coffee into the new filter, the danger is that the coffee will unbeknownst to you stay stuck in the scooper, and that you will think you are pouring in scoop after scoop when in fact nothing is going in. Today to be sure I poked my finger into the mound in the filter until I crunched bottom: I felt the coffee grains go past my first knuckle and a little way to the second—but I added another scoop to be sure.

Filling the carafe with water is not so difficult as measuring the coffee, because the sink is directly under the window, and I can sense the weight of the water; but when I pour the water into the top of the coffeemaker sometimes some streams out and down the sides and onto the counter. But who cares? It's just water. It'll be dry by the time there is light.

Then, back in this living room, I position the chair and make sure my computer is plugged in, since its battery no longer holds a charge. I bought it for $250 from a used-computer store several weeks ago: once it was the sleekest and most desirable of black laptops, now it is practically junk. Someone, not me, has worn away the stippling on the space bar under the resting place of the right thumb, and the upright of the *T* is gone; I've changed the screen colors so that they display dark blue letters against a black background, almost illegible even in the dark, and when I'm ready to start typing I tip the screen towards me, so that it nearly grazes the tops of my prancing fingers. I've always liked the phrase *touch-typing*: I type by touch, staring at, or at least looking steadily at, the fire.

When I lit the fire this morning, a pompadour styling of flame came forward from underneath and swooped back around a half-detached piece of bark. Right now there is one flame near the front that has a purple underpainting but a strong opacity of yellows and oranges and whites: it is flapping like one of those pennants that used to be strung around used-car lots. You don't see those so much anymore: multicolored vinyl triangular flags on cords that hopeful sales managers hung from pole to pole to offer a sense of carnival.

5

Good morning, it's 4:20 a.m.—You know, I used to have trouble sleeping, but now I have much less trouble because I'm getting up at four in the morning. Before five, anyway. I'm so sleepy that I sleep well. For some years I relied on suicidal thoughts to help me go to sleep. By day I'm not a particularly morbid person, but at night I would lie in bed imagining that I was hammering a knitting needle into my ear, or swan-diving off a ledge into a black void at the bottom of which were a dozen sharp, slippery stalagmites. Wearing a helmet and pilot's gear, I would miniaturize myself, and wait for a giant screwdriver to unscrew the hatch at the nose of a bullet. I would be lowered into the control room of the bullet, whereupon the hatch would be screwed tight over me. At a certain moment, I would flick a switch and the gun would fire, throwing me back in my seat. I would shoot out the muzzle and over the sleeping city, following a path towards my own house; I would crash through the window and plunge toward my own head, and when the bullet dove into my brain I would fall asleep.

Now I lie in bed and think a few random things about soil erosion or painting a long yellow strip on the side of a black ship, and because I've gotten up so early, I just fall asleep. The soporific suicidalism peaked several years ago, when we were staying for a few months in San Diego, so that I could "encourage" a group of doctors who were supposed to be revising their textbook. My brain was alive with the nightcrawlerly unfinishedness of the project, and there were four palm trees that I could see from the window of the room that I was using as a temporary office. The palms were beautiful trees in their way, especially as part of a quartet, but there is an intrinsic scrawniness to the palm, which grows like a flaring match, with a little fizzle of green at the top. It is doing only what is absolutely necessary to do to be a tree; and it has big, coarse leaves—intemperate leaves—and the bark shows its years on the outside, so that the tree has no secrets: it doesn't have to die and be cut down before you can date its birth. I would look up at those four trees as I worked, and then at night I would imagine digging my own grave, because it just seemed that it would be so much easier to die than to get those three contentious doctors to contribute their material for the new and heavily revised edition of *Spinal Cord Trauma*. Claire and the children would be fully provided for as long as I was able to craft a way of dying that didn't seem like suicide. But eventually the new edition was written, and then it was copyedited and indexed and published and distributed, and now medical-school students are buying it and underlining things in it, and all is as it should be.

At around four-thirty, sometimes later, the freight-train whistle goes off. At seven I have to get dressed and drop my daughter Phoebe off at school and drive to work. I would like to visit the factory that makes train horns, and ask them how they are able to arrive at that chord of eternal mournfulness. Is it deliberately sad? Are the horns saying, Be careful, stay away from this train or it will run you over and then people will grieve, and their grief will be as the inconsolable wail of this horn through the night? The out-of-tuneness of the triad is part of its beauty. A hundred years ago, a trolley line and two passenger trains came through this town; Rudyard Kipling reportedly stayed here for a week on his way inland to his house in Vermont, where he wrote the *Just So Stories*. "How the Leopard Got His Spots" is a good one. My mother read it to my brother and me, and it changed the way I thought about shadows. There were several places in our yard that offered Kipling's kind of jigsawed shade. The euonymus tree that grew near the edge of our property worked best. Euonymus bark has beautiful fins, and under this low tree I could sit and watch the sunlight break into pieces.

I like deciduous trees, frankly, especially trees with lichen growing on them. I like living in the east, I like old brass boxes with scratches, I like the way fireplaces look when they've held thousands of fires. The fireplace that I'm sitting in front of was built, supposedly, in 1780. How many fires has it held? Two hundred a year times two hundred years: forty thousand fires? I like to burn wood. I've only discovered this recently. Last year, Claire gave me an ax for my birthday, and I began using it to chop up the scrap wood that the contractors piled up where they were reconstructing our slumped barn. If you bring the

ax down really hard, right in the middle of a six-inch
board, the board will break in two longways, and the
grain of the breakage will sometimes detour nicely
around a knothole. Then you can chop across the grain.
Apple boughs are very hard to chop, even the old gray
ones that have lost their bark. You slam away at them
for five minutes and then suddenly, if you hit them just
right, they leap up at you and whack you in the face.
Contractor's scraps burn with many little explosions and
whistling sighs.

When we had burned through most of the scraps, I
called up a wood man and ordered a cord. A cord is a unit
of measure that means "a goodly amount." The wood man
used a large pincering hook to snag the quartered logs off
his truck. He drove off with a pale blue check in his hand,
leaving us with a heap of logs. This heap Claire and I, over
the next week, built into a long, neat edifice against the
barn. You crisscross the logs: three one way, and then
three over those going the other way, and you put each
crisscrossing pile next to the other, and you have to
choose the logs so that the pile will remain stable and not
topple; and you surmount the whole architecture with a
roof made of stray pieces of bark. It takes on an air of

permanency, like a stone wall—so finished seeming that you hesitate before pulling from it the first few logs for burning.

The woodpile quickly became an object of fascination for the duck. She roots in between the logs and bangs at the bark with her beak until some breaks off, to see if there are bugs underneath. Now that everything is frozen, there is much less for her to eat there, but once in the fall I lifted a bottom log for her and she found an ant colony and several worms which she consumed with much lusty beak smacking. She is a dirty eater. She snuffles in mud and grass and then goes over to the plastic wading pool that we set up for her and drinks from it, and streams of dirt flow from her beak as she scoops up the water. When she has found a patch of wet earth or weeds that particularly pleases, she makes a whimpering sound of happiness, as a piglet would at the udder. I had no idea that ducks were capable of such noises. In coloration she resembles a tabby cat.

The other day I pried up a log from the stiff ground and turned it over so that Greta (that's the duck's name) could have a once-over on it before I brought it inside. It's not just that I want to give her a treat; it's also that I don't

want to be bringing termites or strange larvae into the
house. She rooted all over the exposed underside, as if
she were Teletyping a wire-service story on it. Finally she
located, hidden in a crevice, a brown thing that excited
her. She was able to pry it out: it was a frozen slug. Its
slime had grown ice crystals, giving it a kind of fur. I
couldn't tell if it was hibernating or dead. The duck
tumbled it around in her beak and tossed it into the water
(whose icy edges she'd broken earlier), and eventually
much of it went down her gullet. She bobs her head to
work things down into the lower part of her neck, and I
suppose her gizzard goes to work on them there.

6

Good morning, it's 6:08 a.m.—late. When I got up and stood on the landing at the top of the stairs I could see three light effects. One was the white spreadsheet of the moonlight on the floor, and one was more moonlight barred with long banister shadows on the floor downstairs, and one was the hint of pale yellow and blue of dawn arriving beyond the trees. Or maybe it was the glow of the convenience store in the next town. I got up late because I stayed up late working on that thief of time, a website. Nothing so completely sucks an evening away as fiddling with the layout of a website. By the time I was in bed reading "The Men That Don't Fit In" by Robert Service, Claire was asleep in her blue fleece bathrobe and it was eleven o'clock.

But now I'm up and little flames are growing like sedums from the cracks in today's log wall, and I still have a little while before I have to drive Phoebe to school. Every morning the coffee makes me blow my nose, and then I toss the nose-wad into the fire, and it's gone. The fire is like a cheerful dog that waits by the table as you feed it life-scraps.

Our bedroom was still quite dark when I got up. I felt for my glasses on the bedside table in that tender way one uses for glasses, as if one's fingers are antennae, so as not to get smears on them. The smear of a fingerprint makes it impossible to concentrate on anything; it's much worse than the round blur in your vision made by a speck of dust. The glasses made a little clacking sound as I sat up and put them on—oh yeah, baby. The nice thing about putting on your glasses in the dark is that you know you could see better if it were light, but since it is dark the glasses make no difference at all.

My hand seemed to know just where my glasses would be, and this reminded me of something that I noticed about five years ago in a hotel bathroom. I wish I'd taken photographs of all the hotel rooms I've been in. Some of them stay in my head for a while, and some disappear immediately——those many shades of pinky beige. I remember well two of the hotel rooms that Claire and I stayed in on our honeymoon——one a fancy one, and one in an unprosperous little town. There was a bathroom behind an accordion wall in that one.

Claire has just come in to say good-morning. She said that she could tell that I hadn't been up for too long today because of the newer smell of the coffee. She has a good sense of smell. In college there were coed bathrooms; one time she knew that it was I who had surreptitiously peed in the shower stall. Right now she's unhappy that the last American manufacturer of a certain kind of wooden spoon has gone out of business. She saw a woman on the news saying, "This was my life. My grandmother made spoons, my mother made spoons, and now it's finished." Claire likes old people——not just relations, but old people in general. She's become friends with the catty woman down the street, and she is used to the smell of oxygen from oxygen tanks. I'm glad she likes old people because it means that when I get old she will be less likely to be disgusted with me.

I've known Claire for——let me figure it out——twenty-three of my forty-four years. More than half my life I've

loved her. Think of that. We met on the stairs of a
dormitory; I was carrying my bicycle down and she and
her roommate were walking upstairs carrying bags of
new textbooks. We lived on Third North, the third floor
on the north side, a hall of extremely young boys and girls
(so they seem to me now) who, because we all shared a
large bathroom, quickly became chummy. Claire and her
roommate gave cocktail parties every Tuesday at 4:30,
using the floor's ironing board as a bar. I walked out in the
snow with them to buy the liquor: I was twenty-one, and
Pennsylvania had one of those tiresome laws.

When Claire was a little drunk, she would rock
slowly to reggae and her lips would get cold. Her mouth,
however, was warm and her teeth sharp. I cultivated a
rakishly nutty air: I discovered a fine prewar toilet on
the curb and carried it into my room, propping the two-
volume *Oxford English Dictionary* inside. But Claire had
a thing for a very handsome sandy-haired boy named
William. Many had crushes on William because he was
gentle and aloof and had an appealing way of clearing his
throat before he spoke. Rumor had it that his penis was
unusually attractive, but I never saw it. William's father
was a famous surgeon, and one day William borrowed

some thread and showed us how to tie the knots that famous surgeons use on wounds. He never drank. When, maliciously, I tried to slip a little gin in his tonic, he sipped and handed the glass back to me with a reproachful look. I still feel guilty.

Claire had a thing for gentle William, as I say—and then one evening, after one of the ironing-board cocktail parties, she asked me out on a date with her to walk to the cash machine. I said that a walk to the cash machine would be very nice. In those days she wore a thrift-store cashmere coat and soft Italian sweaters and, though her mother pleaded with her, no bra. And her lips were soft, too—much softer and somehow more intelligent than others I'd kissed, and though I hadn't kissed that many lips I'd kissed some.

I went with her to the dentist when she had her wisdom teeth out. Afterward she slept curled for a long time, a small beautiful person; there on her desk in a glass of water were the two enormous teeth. They were like the femurs of brontosauri. How those giant teeth could have fit into her head I don't know.

So this morning when I reached for my glasses, I remembered noticing in a hotel how my hand had gotten better at knowing just where the soap was in an alien shower. My lower mind would hold in its memory a three-dimensional plan of the shower that included the possible perches for the soap: the ledge, the indented built-in soap tray, the near corner, the far corner. I would wash my face, then put the soap down somewhere without thinking about it, then shampoo; and then, still blind from the shampoo, I'd want to wash my lower-down areas, and even though I'd been turning around and around in the shower, I was able to use the north star of the angle of the shower-flow to orient myself, so that without looking I could bend and find the bar of soap under my fingers, often without any groping.

7

Good morning, it's 4:19 a.m., and I can't get over how bright the moon is here. We've lived in Oldfield for over three years now and the brightness of the moon and stars is one of the most amazing things about the place. Even when there's a big chunk taken out of it, as there is now, the moon's light is powerful enough that you can sense, looking out the window, what direction it's coming from. When you look anglingly up, there's this thing high in the sky that you almost have to squint at. The small, high-up moons seem to be the brightest ones.

I fell asleep a little after ten reading a software manual, and now I'm up and waiting for the train whistle. The fire today is made partly of half-charred loggage from yesterday, but mostly from thin apple branches that I sawed up when I got home from work. I tried the ax first and had a heck of a time. But a handsaw will slide right through with wondrous ease, sprinkling handfuls of sawdust out of either side of the cut, like—like I can't think what—like a sower sowing seeds, perhaps. Anyway the fire took to burning so readily that I've had to move my chair back a little so that my legs aren't in pain through the flannel.

The thing that is so great about sitting here in the early morning is that it doesn't matter what I did all yesterday: my mind only connects with fire-thoughts. I have an apple to eat if I want to eat it—picked in the fall and refrigerated in a state of semi-permanent crispness.

The whole dropping-of-the-leaves thing and the coming of winter is one of those gradual processes that becomes harder to believe each year it happens. All those leaves were up there firmly attached to the trees, and they're gone. Now, incredibly, there are *no leaves on the trees.* And not only that, but it's becoming impossible to conceive that there ever would have been leaves on the trees. It's like death, which is also becoming harder and harder for me to understand. How could someone you know and remember so well be dead? My grandmother, for instance. I can't believe that she is dead. I don't mean that I believe in a hereafterly world, I don't. But it does seem puzzling to me that she is now not living.

This year there was a particular moment of leaf-falling that I hadn't encountered before. I went outside at sunrise to feed the duck—this was sometime in October. There was ice in her water when she jumped in: hard pieces of something that she thought might be good to eat but weren't particularly when she tumbled and smacked them around with her beak. While I was waiting for my daughter Phoebe to come out, I began scraping off the thin ice layer on the windshield using my AAA card, and then I heard a leafy rustling a few hundred yards away. I looked in the direction of the sound, expecting to see a coon cat or a fox. What I saw, instead, was a middle-sized, yellow-leafed sugar maple tree. It was behaving oddly: all of its leaves were dropping off at the same time. It wasn't the wind—there was no wind. I stood there for a while, watching the tree denude itself at this unusual pace, and I came up with a theory to explain the simultaneity of the unleaving. The tree was not as tall as some of the other trees—that's the first thing. And it was the first night-freeze of the year. So we can imagine all the twigs of the tree coated with the same thin but tenacious coat of ice that I was encountering on the windshield. Now the sun had risen enough to clear the dense hummock of forest across the creek, and thus sunlight was striking and warming the leaves on this particular tree for the first time since they'd frozen. The night-ice had sheathed the skin, holding the leaf in place, but the freeze had also caused the final rupture in the parenchymatous cells that attached the leaf-stem to its twig: as soon as the ice melted, the leaf fell. I had some confirmation of my theory when I noticed that the leaves on the sunward side of the tree were mainly the ones that were falling.

My son, who is eight, had a plan for the leaves this year. He filled six large kraft-paper bags with them, and saved them in the barn, so that when my brother and sister-in-law came to visit with their children he could make an enormous pile. His plan worked, which is not true of all of his plans. The pile was big and the leaves were dry, not soggy, and my sister-in-law and I took lots of pictures of smiling children leaping around piles of leaves and flinging them in the air, and I had that moment of slight fear when I knew the future. I knew that we would remember this moment better than other perhaps worthier or more representative moments because we were taking pictures of it. The duck hovered near the rake, hoping that we would get down to a slimy underlayer where the worms lived. But there wasn't one.

I found out yesterday that one of the town elders has died. He sounded perfectly fine over the phone when I talked to him in November—gravelly-voiced but fine. When I was taking out the garbage yesterday, walking up the ramp that leads into the barn, I suddenly imagined this aged man turning from a living human being to skull and bones—and I was amazed in the same way that I'm amazed when the leaves fall and we're left with skeletal trees every year. Really I'm glad my grandparents were cremated. I don't like the idea that their skulls would be around somewhere. Better and more dignified for them to be completely parceled out.

8

Good morning, it's 4:50 a.m.—I just took such a deep bite of red apple that it pushed my lower lip all the way down to where the lip joins up with the chin. There is a clonk point there, and a good apple can do that, push your lower lip down to its clonk point. Sometimes you think for a moment that you're going to get stuck in the apple because you can't bite down any farther. But all you have to do is push the apple a little to the left—or pull it to the right—and let the half-bitten chunk break off in your mouth. If you do it slowly, it sounds like a tree falling in the forest. Then start chewing.

Phoebe said something yesterday on the way to school that I thought was very true. While I was finishing

feeding the duck, she came out in her perfectly ironed
blue jeans, carrying a piece of toast in her mittens and
crouching like a Sherpa beneath the load of her backpack.
She's fourteen. We both got in the car, and I turned the
heater on full. It roared and hurled out a blast of icy air.
Phoebe held a mitten over her mouth and nose and said,
"It's cold, Dad, it's cold." I said, "You're not kidding it's
cold—it's *really* cold."

As I took hold of the steering wheel, I made an
exaggeratedly convulsive noise of frozenness, and Phoebe
looked over and saw that I was hatless. Then she noticed
that my hat—a tweed hat with a silk inner band—was
stuffed down near the hand brake. It had been in the car
all night, cooling down. She reached for it, and in that
abrupt way that people have when they're trying to
conserve warmth, she held it out to me. "Put this on,"
she said.

The thick tweed looked tempting, but I knew better
and I said, "If I put this on I'm going to freeze."

She took the hat back from me and held it over the
heater vents for a few seconds. "Try it now," she said.

The heater, as it turned out, had not warmed the hat

to any perceptible degree: the silk inner band was a ring of ice and my head recoiled at the chill. I said: "Yow, yes, that's going to be better."

"You've got to get cold to get warm," Phoebe said.

Now that is the truth. That is so true about so many things. You learn it first with sheets and blankets: that the initial touch of the smooth sheets will send you shivering, but their warming works fast, and you must experience the discomfort to find the later contentment. It's true with money and love, too. You've got to save to have something to spend. Think of how hard it is to ask out a person you like. In my case, Claire asked me to go on a date to the cash machine, so I didn't actually have to ask her. Still, her lips were cold, but her tongue was warm.

By the time I dropped Phoebe off and gave her a dollar for a snack, my hat was as comfortably situated on my head as if it had hung on the coat tree all night.

Henry was building a Mars city when I got home from work. He went upstairs and came out of his room with an enormous Rubbermaid storage container full of Lego. It seemed bigger than he could handle. Each Lego piece is as light as a raisin, but they become heavy in the aggregate.

"Do you need some help with that?" I asked him.

"No, thanks, I think I can do it," said Henry.

"That's certainly a lot of Lego," I said.

"Dad, you should see how I get it up the stairs. It takes me about an hour." He stepped down each step very slowly, his heels treading on the edges of his too-long sweatpants. "Sometimes I get in hard situations where I'm balanced on one toe. It's not very pleasant."

I've turned the top half-log over—it looks like a glowing side of beef now.

9

Good morning, it's 4:23 a.m.——I have this ability to use bad dreams to wake myself up when I need to be up. I can just tell myself a time and a bad dream will come and get me just when I need it to. For instance, what woke me this morning at four o'clock was a dream about a low, bullish sort of pig that grunted around. When the pig lifted its head from the grass and saw me, it went very still and changed color from brown to a dark purple. I got up and peed and got back into bed, but I knew I was up for the morning then. I have a general theory about bad dreams which I think is revolutionary. My theory is that they are most often simply the result of the body's need to wake up the mind using the only tools it has available, most often in order to pee. The mind is unconscious, in a near coma, but the body has received reports of a substantial accumulation of hot urine belowdecks. The body is getting insistent calls and memos describing the gravity of the hot urine situation, and passing it up to the low-brain, and the low-brain is putting in calls to the high-brain, but the high-brain's phone is unplugged because it is asleep. What is the low-brain to do? It has three options: laughter, arousal, or fear. All three will elevate the heart rate, but laughter and arousal are, especially if the high-brain really wants to keep sleeping for a last ten or fifteen minutes, less dependable. Fear it must be, then. The low-brain looks on the monitor at the images that float by in an unstoppable stream of coolant. They are, as always, absurd and pointless. Any one of them will do. He seizes one at random—it happens to be of a small faun-colored pig in the yard—and he injects a special fear-chemical into it and lets it go, and suddenly it is a frightening dark-purple pig with murderous eyes. And if that doesn't work, then there will be gray zombies hiding in tree stumps, glossy-green tidal waves, stairways that narrow down and drip mud, suffocating sweaters that you knit yourself and can't escape from, tough Eskimos who want to kidnap your children, and so on, all coming at the end of sequences of mindless innocence—and the breathing elevates, the heart begins to pound, the eyes snap open. My contention is that the simple need to pee accounts for over half of the bad dreams that human beings experience, and it certainly accounts for my pig dream this morning.

The fire had some trouble today. I balled up six sheets of the *News Herald* and laid over them two torn-off flaps from a cardboard box, with a crumpled Cheez-Its container laid over that, and at first the fire was healthy— so healthy was it in fact that I burned my sock when I looked away for a moment. Not my toe—just the white sock, which now has a rough black charred area at the tip. When the fire died down I stuffed a paper-towel tube deep into the orange otherworldly cavern between two lower logs: quantities of gray smoke issued from one end of the tube as the other end burned. But then it all died down again. This happens sometimes. When it does, you must take a moment to appreciate the unburning fire. It's still hot—it still has the means of its own regeneration. Blow on it several times, long steady gulf-streams of oxygen, and a flame sprat will pop up again somewhere. Then adjust the logs slightly to give that flame some encouragement, and the fire is loping off on its own again.

So now let me say a little about this room, our living room. It looks like a real living room, I must say, and I like sitting in here because it is clean. My office is filled with my junk. I can't think about anything but work in there, and I don't want to think about work. Here there are five windows with thin white curtains, and each window has twelve panes of glass. The muntins—those little wooden pieces that hold the panes—look narrow and fragile, but they've been there for a long time. The room has looked more or less like this, with molding going around the wall three feet off the floor and warped pine planks, for over two hundred years, which is a long time. We have been here only three years, though. There is a couch in the room, and a triangular corner cupboard, and various chairs—nothing in the room is new, everything has been glued or repaired at some time in its life. Some of it is from Claire's family, some from mine. The oriental rug came from my parents, who bought it for four hundred dollars around 1970. My parents were then big fans of oriental rugs—less so now because their interests have changed. Their most extravagant acquisition was a tiger rug—an oriental rug with a life-size hieratic tiger lifting its paw in the middle and incomprehensible designs running around the edge. They bought it for nine hundred dollars. It was too valuable to have on the floor: it hung on the wall in the front hall. One day when I was twelve or so, we were doing a family housecleaning, and I got interested in the idea of beating all the rugs. I took the little rugs out and hit them with a broom handle, and then I beat the tiger rug, imagining that the dust particles that poofed out had magical powers—and when I was done I hung it out over the railing on the front porch. I said to myself that I was hanging it there because I wanted it to "air out," but really it was that I wanted people on our street to see that we had this very unusual and expensive rug. Towards dusk I heard an odd clink. I went out on the front porch. A car with a rusty trunk was driving off. The rug was gone, stolen. My mother wept. She would have it now if I hadn't wanted to watch the dust puff out of it.

10

Good morning, it's 3:37 a.m., and it's just me here in the dark. I had a tussle with the coffeemaker just now. Claire warned me last night that she'd put its components in the dishwasher. "That won't confuse you early in the morning?" she asked. I said nah, and it shouldn't have. I unclamped the dishwasher door and allowed it to fall and bounce a little—the springs made their sproinging sound. I'm always happy to open a dishwasher, curious to see what Dead Sea Scrolls await within. I pulled on the top cage of dishes, feeling how smoothly its rollers rolled in the dark, making a sort of soft thunder as the extenders slid out and a little jingle when they reached their limit. And as soon as I began feeling up the dishes to try to find the filter basket, I encountered, faintly lingering there and

radiating upward, the living traces of warmth from
the long-completed dishwashing cycle—hints of heat
persisting seven hours after I cranked the dial to Normal
Wash. How could the machine have held the warmth this
far into the early morning? Insulation, of course—that
was the easy answer. But there was a further reason: in
the upturned bottoms of all the mugs were shallow
tidepools of warm water. These residual heat-sinks, along
with all the molecules of agitated ceramic in the plates
and mugs and all the forky forests of silverware, worked
like radiators. And the pools of water are important in
another way, too: if you open the dishwasher and you
aren't sure at a glance whether the dishes in it are clean or
dirty, you can know their status for certain by checking
to see whether the mugs hold these cupped pools, since
when you upend a dirty mug and put it in the cage, it
may be wet, but there won't be water collected in
its concavity because you will have carried it to the
dishwasher right side up, only turning it upside down
when you place it into the angled outside edge of the
upper cage.

I found the carafe easily, and the filter basket was

behind the carafe. I pulled out one of the mugs. But where was the plastic snap-on lid that went on the top of the carafe? I groped my way around the whole dishwasher twice, methodically, before I finally found it leaning under a bowl. And then I had a terrible time snapping the top into place. I was pressing so hard that I worried that I might shear off the plastic pins on either side of the flange on the top flap, and that's when I broke down and switched on the light switch—but it has a rheostat, thanks to our deaf electrician, and I was able to switch it on very low, just enough to be sure that I wasn't shearing off the pins, and when the plastic top clinked into place I turned the light right off and finished up in the dark. The question is, Will that eruption of incandescence make a difference? Can I regain my early-morning consciousness? Everything is different because of everything else, and yet I feel, now safely installed in front of a healthy fire before four o'clock, that it didn't make a bit of difference. My eye has reverted to its night mode without any trouble, and I have the same hollow, sleep-deprived feeling in my head that I always have—a feeling that is precious to me.

I started today's fire with a crumpled-up potato

bag—one of those bags with the window made of a crisscross of open cords. It burned like a bastard and lit some dead apple branches, and with the further help of a Triscuit box and an empty cardboard spool of white ribbon, the flame-front moved up to take control of the upper-tier logs. Striking the match was, in fact, a more searing light experience than turning on the kitchen light. And think of that word, *struck,* which stores within it the old form of fire lighting: we now swipe a match as we swipe a charge card through a machine that will read its magnetic stripe, whereas once, before matches, we must truly have struck a flint. And maybe the early matches were things you did whack against something, as you would strike two flints together, rather than swiping them, though I doubt it. As I remember, the hardboiled detective novels have characters who "scratch" a match, which is a good way of saying it. Diamond "Strike on Box" matches these are, Made in the USA, according to an emblem on the front.

Just now I stretched, looking over to my left at a table that is now in darkness but during the day holds a coffee-table book of Wayne Thiebaud paintings, including a very good painting of bowls of soup, some pumpkin, some pea. While I stretched, thinking of the soup bowls, my hand strayed under my pajama top and my middle finger found its way into my belly button where it discovered some lint. I rolled the lint into a tube, as one does, and having done so, I became curious about what such a tube would look like if it burned. I tossed it into one of the spaces between the coals. It went orange for a moment, fattened, and then darkened. It is still there now but it will be lost when I stir the coals.

Claire told me last night that Lucy, the frail but funny woman who lives on our street, has had to go into the hospital. She's going to be okay, but the woman who helps Lucy was trying to find a home for Lucy's pets. Claire was wondering whether we should take one of the cats. I see that it would be a good thing to do but it seems to me that our current cat gets into terrible fights with neighbor cats already, and he's had a major blow this year as a result of the arrival of the duck. Greta, although not very bright in some ways, is shrewd about cats. What you do is you walk up to the cat slowly, as if you want to say hello, and when the cat tentatively extends its nose in the willing-to-sniff-

and-be-sniffed stance, you peck at him sharply. Then, when the shocked cat turns to walk away, his ears back, his feelings and nose hurt, lunge at him again and peck him directly on or near his anus. That makes him gallop off—for no animal likes to be pecked on the anus by a duck.

Here is, since it has come up again, how we got the duck. Phoebe went to camp this summer—a camp that had llamas, goats, small noisy pigs, and ducks. The ducks had ducklings, and Phoebe called to tell us that there was going to be a lottery, the winner of which would take home a duck. Could she enter the lottery? There were six hundred children at the camp; although I hesitated, I thought it was all right to say yes to the lottery because the chance of our ending up with the duck was tiny. Only four families said yes to the lottery, however, and there were, it turned out, six ducklings. Having "won," Phoebe picked the smallest one—small but, she thought, perky, and we put her in a cardboard box and drove it —her—home. And now we have this brown duck who has enriched our lives considerably. One cat and one duck is enough, however.

The difficulty with the duck in the winter is that the hose is frozen. It is still out there somewhere under the snow-piles that the plow has made, and it will reappear in the spring—but it has disappeared for now. Up till the first blizzard we were filling a plastic wading pool for Greta to use. When the water was fresh she dove and flapped her wings underwater to rinse off her underwing area, lunging forward so hard that unless she turned her head she would bonk into the far side of the pool. We also walked with her down to the creek, where she was happy rooting in the mud. Even after it had snowed we walked with her down the hill once or twice so that she could splash in the very cold creek water. Her yellow feet are unsuited to snow; she has trouble climbing any hill, and yet she flies only to signal that she is hungry.

But now that it is iron-cold, cold enough that we worry about how she manages at night, fluffed in with her cedar shavings, even with the blanket over the doghouse and the snow on the blanket, she has not been immersed in any sort of water for weeks. I hope her feathers don't lose their insulative properties when she can't bathe. Her feet, which you would think would be vulnerable to frostbite when she stands on the ice, seem unaffected. When one foot begins to feel intolerably cold, she just pulls it up into her feathers and stands balanced on the other. Then she switches.

11

Good morning, it's 4:45 a.m. Yesterday my son and I got haircuts from Sheila in town. I like her because she's fast and she doesn't care that I have what Claire calls a "roundabout," meaning that I'm well on my way to being bald. Nor does she want to give my son a shelf haircut. She's a person who just likes cutting people's hair. There you have it—just snipping locks all day long and sweeping the piles into garbage bags. My son gets a solemn expression when he's having a haircut. I looked at him in the mirror, sitting with his wet hair in the big salon chair with the white clerical collar on him—eight years old, noticeably taller than last time, with good straight shoulders and a straight back—and I wanted to make low animal noises, growlings, of love for him. I can't call him pet names like "Dr. Van Deusen" anymore in public, he has forbidden me. I now must call him simply Henry. Henry it is. I asked Sheila what she thought of the siding that was going up on the old Congregational church in town. She nodded approvingly and said, "Low maintenance."

Sometimes if Sheila's closed or booked up, Henry and I go to Ronnie's barbershop. The first year we lived here, we went to Ronnie's father, also named Ronnie, a man who nodded and pursed his lips as he snipped. The father retired and the son took over. The son scowls all the time; he's one of those people whose mouth falls into a scowl, although in fact he's fairly upbeat. He uses his father's old-fashioned cash register, which makes a ringing sound when you push down the keys. But it's a very long wait in Ronnie's shop, because his prices are low and he gets a lot of business from the military bases nearby. I don't like watching these army people get their hair cut. They want it "skinned" and flat-topped. Their heads rise up off of thick necks and they narrow at the top like medium-range missiles, and as Ronnie uses the shaver on them, folds of back-of-head skin begin to reveal themselves. The back of a man's head is not meant to be seen: there is something repulsive, almost evil, about the place where the skull meets the top of the spine. Old scars, too— Ronnie's shaver's dispassionate teeth move back and forth over a white, C-shaped scar, grinding away the hair.

I asked Ronnie why people want their hair so short, and he said it was convenience. "People don't want to spend time with their hair." Ronnie is mistaken, I think. These men are self-primpers. Every two weeks they are willing to drive all the way to Oldfield and wait for an hour in a chair, staring at their enormous square knees, insisting that their hair be as short as it can possibly be; whereas I get mine cut, and then I forget about it for five months. They seem to enjoy the prickliness— you see them fondling their skulls when they walk out the door. Marines, so Ronnie told me, generally want their hair mown shorter than any other group of military men. They want to look like penile tubes of warmongeringness. I basically want nothing to do with all men except my son, my father, and a few others. Robert Service, the poet, I like. Anyway, that's why Henry and I usually go to have our haircuts at Sheila's.

12

Good morning, it's 5:07 a.m. I'm snoring a lot, and it's keeping Claire awake. She used to say that it was her bedside light that bothered me, but it's gone beyond that now. Probably I snore because I have more fat on the end of my epiglottis, making it floppier.

My grandfather was a great snorer. In his youth, he had ambitions to find a cure for some major disease, which brought him to medical school, and he ended up a research pathologist specializing in fungal diseases of the nose and brain. When I was fifteen, he began paying me to help him proofread his gigantic and wondrously expensive book, *Fungal Disease in Humans*. My grandmother had finally said, after twenty years of doing proofreading and correspondence for him, that she'd had enough. I became one of the few teenagers who could spell *rhinoentomophthoromycosis*—"rhino" because the malady begins in the nose. A number of the diseases that my grandfather studied had first appeared in the early nineteen-fifties after overeager pharmacologists, wanting to believe that steroids were the new miracle drugs, administered them in huge doses, sometimes in African and South American countries. Dosed with a sufficiently heavy course of some corticosteroids, one's immune system stops functioning, and then the hyphae, or creepers, of normally innocent organisms like bread mold take root and grow through the veins and arteries and into the brain, causing blockages and dead places. The pictures of the doomed sufferers are horrible.

My grandfather's other textbook was a compendium of tips and tricks for doing better postmortem examinations, copiously illustrated by a nice man who loved houseplants, and printed on special paper that could be rinsed if you got blood and gook on it. The way to make steady money in the textbook business is to bring out a new edition of your book every two years, whether it needs it or not. Otherwise your book competes with all the used copies of your book that are available for resale. I helped my grandfather with these successive editions, and then, after my job-hunting leads didn't pan out, he got me a position at the publishing company that had brought out his books. And now twenty years later what am I? I'm an editor of medical textbooks. The job pays seventy thousand dollars a year and it isn't terribly difficult. Of course doctors are smart in many ways, but a lot of them are also, in my experience, silly credulous people who need to be told what to think by a textbook, until a different textbook tells them to think differently.

Once when I was just married, I read an Agatha Christie and two Dick Francises, and I thought I should get up early and write a murder mystery about fungal diseases. I imagined a plot like an elaborate machine—like one of those works of mechanical art in airports, in which billiard balls move around on wire tracks, turning windmills and setting off chimes. I filled a silver glass—one of a pair that had been a wedding present—with cold water, and I took a piece of soft wheat bread from out of the bag, and I went to a chair by a window, where I sat looking at the streetlit sunrise, and tried to write about fungus-related death. The condensation on the silver water glass made patterns that I studied closely: it grew a fuzz of tiny droplets, like a reindeer's antler, and then one droplet would break ranks and join with another, and suddenly a bigger dome of a drop, which had sucked in some of its surrounding fuzz and become too heavy to hold its place on the silver surface, slid down an inch, then gathered more strength and, changing direction to avoid an invisible point of resistance, slid another inch. Eventually there were five or six of these trails, and as I sipped the water the lowering of the level of the liquid would influence the texture of the droplets and the trails on the outer surface.

So I sat looking out at the dim world, eating wheat bread and drinking cold water, hoping to come up with a first chapter, where the dead body is discovered. I wrote fourteen pages. Then Claire and I began to notice a puzzlingly sweetish smell in our apartment. It got worse. We told the building manager that we suspected that a raccoon had died on the roof. The manager walked the roof and found nothing. Then came the hideous black flies, the biggest I'd ever seen. The woman next door stuffed a towel in the crack under her door to block the stench. We thought maybe the solid-waste plant down the road had had a mishap. But it turned out that the man below us had died. I thought, I don't want to write a murder mystery with a plot like a machine; I don't want a corpse lying there pushing a little imaginary world into gear.

The Postmortem Handbook, my grandfather's small but steady seller, was translated into Spanish. He believed that what the world needed, above all, was more autopsies. He told us this at Christmas and he told us this at Thanksgiving; he told us this while sitting on a deck chair cruising up the Rhine. Better diagnoses, handier surgeons, wiser doctors, happier patients, all would result from more autopsies. In his will he ordered that an autopsy be performed on his body, as indeed it was. But once he said to me: "Fluorescent light is bad for the eyes. Pick a life that gets you outdoors." I work all day in fluorescent light; it isn't so bad. But maybe that's why I crave this fire, which is hissing nicely after I stuffed in more of yesterday's cardboard box.

My grandfather was a determined walker, and he sang Purcell songs rather breathlessly while he walked—"I'll Sail upon the Dog-star" and "I Attempt from Love's Sickness to Fly-hi-hi-high in Vain." Later he grew vague and didn't sing anymore, and he began advocating compulsory world disarmament and walking up to smokers in restaurants saying, "Do you enjoy killing yourself?" He continued to practice the piano, however—he played a certain Chopin E-minor prelude over and over in the basement. When my grandmother broke her back and was in bed wondering whether to call the ambulance, my grandfather retreated downstairs to perform Chopin's E-minor prelude several times. As the rest of his mind closed up shop, the musical node carried on.

Once when I was fourteen I arrived at my grandparents' house after twelve hours on a bus. We sat down to dinner. I politely asked my grandfather how his medical work was coming along. "I'm considering whether I should embark on a new research program," he said. "It seems to me that an effective cure for the facial lesions of adolescence would be a contribution to humanity. I notice for instance that you have a number of acne pustules there on your forehead, and on your nose, and I wonder whether you think this disease might yield a fruitful program of research." I said, "Well, yes." Then came the dear, nervous laugh from my grandmother.

13

Good morning, it's 5:36 a.m. I'm finding that a flat slab of junk mail dropped in the mail-slot created by two hot logs can sometimes get an unwilling fire to take the next step. Or try one of those enclosures for lightbulbs—slide that easy flammability into the spot where you wish the fire to move. This morning when I woke up I peed and then, inexplicably, I got back in bed and lay there for a while thinking about driving a speedboat off the watery edge of the world. It seemed to me, as I lay there awake, that the world was indeed flat, and as I reached the edge of it and saw the enormous glossy curve of ocean turn the corner and fall away I sped up. It was like going over Niagara Falls in a barrel. My boat began falling, and as it fell it turned, but I held on to the steering wheel so as not

to become separated from it. I fell towards a region of
mists that I thought was the bottom, and I prepared to be
dashed to pieces on the rocks, but no, I had fallen off
the edge of the flat world, and the world was fairly thick:
I was passing through the mists in a region that smelled
like a salty shower, where the ocean began to pour past
the inner molten earth-sandwich. The steam dried away
finally and I tumbled past a cross-section of semi-plastic
moltenness, and then, as I kept falling, I blew through the
mists again, which cooled my hull, and I rose up past
another waterfall that mirrored the one over which I had
fallen; and then the bow of my boat, its progress slowing,
reached a turning point about twenty feet in the air and
I fell down with a slap on the gray, choppy ocean on the
other side of the earth. Fighting the waters there that
wanted to push me back off, I drove the boat to shore.
Everything was more or less normal, and I ate at a
Bickford's and left a generous tip, but I wanted to go
home to the "real" side of the earth, the side I was born
on, and the phone system on the underside, where I was,
didn't reach through to the other side: so after a night in a
motel I drove my boat back out to the edge of the ocean
and hurled myself and my boat back out into the void, far

enough that, with the stars at my back, I had a good view of the cataract falling off into the lava layers, and then, like an adept skateboarder, I flipped up the stern of my boat at the point of highest rising and slap-landed neatly back in our ocean. I was home in a few hours.

That's what I lay there thinking about. Then I got up and came down here and made the coffee. Sometimes when I imagine driving off the end of the earth—it isn't a subject I take up every day but it does recur—I consider what it would be like to go out for a little stroll in the direction of the setting sun and then trip on a rock, and, oh, heavens, I've fallen off a cliff. And then as I fall I look around—wait, this is not just any cliff, I seem to have fallen off the edge of the flat earth. In my descent I try to keep my wits about me and look downward, where I'm falling, and there I see, coming towards me, a huge burning dome of fusion: the sun. Yes indeed, I'm falling towards the sun, which when it sets goes down here past the edge of the world for the night and rests, keeping the lava bubbly near the middle of things. Fortunately I've got my magical sunglasses on, so that when I plunge into the sun, which roars like a locomotive, it isn't too bad on the eyes, and then I'm squirted out again, and I fall—i.e., rise—past rocks and roots until I'm almost at the edge of the underworld, and there I grab a root and hang on, dangling, and pull myself up so that my chin is over the edge, and I have a brief chance to survey its features. It is a grassy place with some trees and a new housing development going up, each house with a large pseudo-Palladian window over the front door. And then the root gives way and I tumble away back through the set sun: down once again becomes up and I am back on the grassy verge where I began my walk.

Claire and I took a walk yesterday afternoon along the place where the trolley to West Oldfield used to go. When we started, there was still plenty of afternoon light left, and then the slow-roasting orange clouds began, and by the time we reached the little cemetery where you can see through to the lake, the light had an impoverished glow of the sort that induces one's retinas to give extra mileage to any color because the total wattage of light is so radically reduced. Where the snow had gone away, the tan layer of needles on the ground sang out with a boosted pallor, and a mitten-shaped patch of cream-colored lichen on a gravestone waved at me in the gloom and made me want to have been a person who devoted his life to the study of lichens. I told Claire that I was having lichen-scientist thoughts, wishing I had become a lichen man, and she nodded. She's heard me say it before.

I'm burning a bunch of little pinecones now that I gathered on the walk. One of the joys of life, I think, is trying to decipher the name on a gravestone as it is transmitted through the dense foliage of blue-green gravestone lichen. Some people clean off the grave-growths with chemicals and wire brushes, a mistake.

Where have I seen that interesting blue-green lichen color recently? Yesterday morning it was—no, day before yesterday—when I opened the hood of our Mazda minivan in order to replenish the tank of windshield-washer fluid. I'd turned on the car to warm it up, and I'd pressed the button that activates the rear-window heater—a stave of long wires elegantly arranged like the plectrum of a hardboiled-egg slicer, buried in the glass, which melts the ice with surprising efficiency—and then I pulled the hood release and heard the hood spring free. I propped it up on its cold rod. The windshield fluid is stored in an L-shaped tank that has a representation of a windshield wiper's swath molded into it. It was down to the dregs, squirted dry. That's not safe. When the trucks salt the roads, the white smear of salt solution on the windshield sometimes catches the glare of the risen sun and obscures the road entirely, forcing me to poke my head out the window to see where we're going. The plastic was cold and inflexible, its edges slightly painful to the fingers. I poured the pink liquid in. The engine, idling, trembled its hoses. When the tank was full, I snapped the lid back on and pulled the hood prop from its oval hole and, lowering it, pushed it into the metal prongs that wait in the gutterish area where the hood's shape fits. And then, just before I let the hood drop shut, I noticed that the battery had grown some lovely turquoise exudate, electrical lichen, around one of its poles.

It isn't clear to me why I grew up to be someone who can spell rhinoentomophthoromycosis, and yet whose knowledge of car repair extends only as far as replenishing the windshield-wiper fluid. When I was a teenager, I took off and put back on as much of my ten-speed bicycle as I could, soaking the wheel bearings in gasoline overnight and then packing them back in their tracks with fresh, pale grease. Ah, what a keen pleasure it is to glide ticking down a leafy street with fresh grease on one's wheel bearings. But I've never taken the next step and begun tinkering with cars.

Come to think of it, the bicycle was the beginning of my end-of-the-earth thoughts: I'd be on a trip down a long straight road, and the road would become steeper and steeper until finally it was plunging vertically down and the stars would come out around me, and I'd fall past the strata, and then somewhere along the way a road would form on the side of the cliff and I would land on it and begin bicycling as hard as I could up what became a very steep hill, and when I finally crested the top of the hill I would be in the underworld.

14

Good morning, it's 5:25 a.m.——once I told a doctor from France that I was able to wake myself up at a preset time with the help of nightmares, and he said that his father had been a soldier who had taught him that if you want to wake up at, say, five in the morning, you simply bang your head five times on the pillow before you close your eyes, and you will wake up at five. "But how do you manage five-thirty?" I asked the doctor with a crafty look. He said that in order to wake at five-thirty you just had to do something else with your head, like jut your chin a little, to signify the added fraction, and your sleeping self would do the math for you. I've tried it and it works except that it's much harder to go to sleep because your head has just been hit repeatedly against the pillow.

Incredible: I'm forty-four years old. What's incredible about it is that my children are eight and fourteen years old, still here living with us. I'm driving Phoebe to her school every morning, after she irons her blue jeans. Only a few months ago I realized that when my father was the age I am now he had already lost me—that is, I'd already gone off to college and moved away. My parents were twenty-three when I was born, which would mean that my father drove down with me to college and bought me my first typewriter when he was only forty-one. What did it feel like to lose me? Maybe not so bad. Maybe by the time it happens you're used to the idea.

The Olivetti electric typewriter that my father bought me was designed—this was in the seventies—in the high-Italian way, like a Bugatti from that era, very clean, no sharp corners but no unnecessary aerodynamicism either. It made a fine swatting sound when one of its keys hit the paper. A week after I got it, I masked over all the letters with black electrician's tape, and that was how I learned to type. I took it with me to France and typed French papers there with it. Six years later it was stolen from Claire's apartment, when thieves

came in through the fire escape. They stole her miniature
TV and her roommate's speakers, too. I find it remarkable
that my father was buying me a farewell typewriter when
he was younger than I am now.

Last night I washed my son's hair, thinking what I
always think: How many years will be left before I have
no child young enough to wash his or her hair? Phoebe
takes long showers now and of course washes her own
hair. The loss is enough to make you lose composure—
I'm not kidding. The dawn sky is now visible: the snow
is a very light blue rather than grey. Yes, grey with an
e—that's one of those English spellings that I accept
(*aeroplane* isn't bad either), and not just because I learned
to read it on the boxes of Earl Grey tea that my mother
had. When spelled with an *e*, *grey* half hides the wide,
crude sound of the *a* behind the obscuring mists of the *e*.
It's rare for a one-syllable word to have so much going on.

I once saw the earl of Grey on *The Merv Griffin Show,*
an afternoon program hosted by the always cheerful and
always tanned Merv Griffin. The earl of Grey had three
things to say: one, that you can't make good tea in a
microwave; two, that the water shouldn't be boiling but
just on the verge; and three, that he wished that Twinings

had trademarked the phrase *Earl Grey,* which was used by everyone. The poor man had lost his name.

And it was on *The Merv Griffin Show,* as well, that I watched a father-and-son act in which the son, who was about seven or eight, climbed up a ladder and got into a small chair welded to the top of a long pole. The father balanced this pole on his hand, his foot, and then lifted it and placed it on his chin. But here something went wrong. The father had never been on TV before, one suspects, and he was nervous, and the lights onstage were brighter and hotter than the lights that he had rehearsed under, and he knew that he had a shorter time than usual, only two or three minutes, to do his act, before they cut away to the commercial. So his face was sweating more than it normally did—it was in fact dripping. He and his son were both wearing leopard-pattern caveman outfits—crazy-looking getups with belts and shoulder straps as I remember. Perhaps the wife, who made the costumes, thought it was cute.

The man threw back his head and got his chin into position under the chin-cup at the end of the pole that held his son in the air and set it in place, and spread his arms. But then I saw two rapid jerky adjustments—

maybe the son was more nervous too and fidgeted for a moment—and one of the movements made the chin-cup slide off the man's unusually slippery chin. It slipped down his neck, and his neck tendons became dozens of individual cords as he grimaced, and the pole continued to slip until it came to rest in the hollow just above his collarbone, where he held it by tightening his neck muscles so that the pole wouldn't drive right into the soft tissue there. He held that, quivering, for a few seconds, until the orchestra made the sound of triumph, and the applause came, and then he lifted the pole off, brought it down, and the son jumped into his arms and the two of them took a bow in their matching leopard-skin caveman outfits.

Anyway, I gave Henry a bath, and saw all of his forehead, as you do when your child is in the bath— all that high, smooth forehead, as I rinsed out the shampoo, and I pointed towards the back of the tub, meaning "Look way back," so that his head would tip back enough for me to rinse the shampoo from the hair just above his forehead, and I saw his young face, trusting me not to drip water in his eyes, his mouth chapped below one side of his lower lip because he sticks the tip of his tongue out and to the side when he is concentrating, which is a genetic behavior that he inherited from my father-in-law (who puts his tongue at the corner of his mouth and bites it while performing some act of minor manual dexterity; their heads and ears are similarly shaped, too)—and I thought, I've got only a few years of Henry being a small boy. Even now when he stretches his legs out, his feet push against the tap-end of the tub. I remember how proud Phoebe was to be able to touch both ends of the tub, too—"Nice growing!" I said to her. And I even remember how proud I was myself to touch both ends of the tub. Generations of people grow to a point where they touch both ends of the tub. This is all too much for me.

15

Good morning, it's 4:04 a.m. and I made the coffee very strong this morning. Two extra scoops in the dark. The cat wanted to be fed, but the cat rule is not before six-thirty, otherwise there will come days, I guarantee it, when I will want to sleep and the cat will want to eat at what will have become his accustomed time. When we're still asleep and he thinks that it is breakfast time, he slides his claws into the fabric along the side of the mattress and then plucks the bed like a giant harp.

Passing through the dining room, after an eye-moistening crunch of apple, I saw a coppery flare of sloshing liquid where my coffee mug must be. Once again I thought it must be moonlight—moonlight in the morning coffee—but no, there is no moon available. And then I recognized, by experimenting with where I held the coffee, that I was seeing a liquid reflection of the light from my new friend, the little green bulb in the smoke detector.

The mug of coffee rests on the top of the ashcan, and it gets hot on the side that is near the fire. But it stays cool on the side I sip from. This particular mug has a blue stripe around it and a small chip in the sipping area. Each time I take a sucking mouthful of tepid coffee I have the sharp-edged, chalky, chipped-ceramic experience as well, a good combination.

I've got my eyes closed now. The flames make semaphoring rhythms against my eyelids. An itch just made a guest appearance on my cheek, in the foothills of my beard—as the fire gets hotter it can make your face itch—and I noticed that I've gotten into the habit of using my tongue to prop my cheek from underneath, in order to stretch the skin a little and establish a solid base against which to scratch. I wonder now when I first began countering the force of my finger-scratch with tongue pressure through the cheek. Years ago, it must have been; I've kept no record. Once I had a briefcase that got a long scratch in it. I was looking for a job after college, and my father, in whose house I was then living (my parents having separated a year or two earlier), bought me a hand-sewn briefcase made of dark leather—not the lawyerly kind with the expandable bellows but a simpler design with two leather handles that slid down into the recesses in the sides of the central compartment. The briefcase sat on a chair in the middle of my room—every day I woke up and saw it there and was made happy by it. In it was a file with all four of my unfinished poems and another with my résumé and several more empty folders ready for the time when I would have more things to file. My father was at work by nine, so I didn't see him in the morning, but he would leave notes for me—NEW BOX OF CHEERIOS, a note would say, in his fast but calligraphy-influenced printing, with a late-Victorian arrow pointing to the unopened Cheerios box, which was displayed at just the right angle to the paper. Next to the Cheerios was a bunch of bananas (often), and he would draw a hand with an extended index finger calling attention to that. NOTE FRESH BANANAS! the message would say, and the exclamation point would have its own drop shadow. I wish I had every morning note my father ever wrote me. I have some, I think, I hope.

So I would get up around ten-thirty and take a shower and talk to Claire on the phone, and then I would go out into the world with my new briefcase to seek my fortune, which involved walking around downtown for about an hour until I got hungry. One day I went to a cafeteria to have a hamburger. I was sitting down at the table with my briefcase in one hand and my tray holding a hamburger and a medium root beer, coleslaw, coffee, and a piece of pecan pie in the other, when the cup of root beer somehow tipped over and gushed into my new briefcase. I used some foul language and poured the root beer out of the briefcase into the tray. I took little pleasure in my lunch, although the mushrooms on the hamburger were quite good. When I was done, I called my father from a pay phone and told him what had happened. He said to go to Paul's Shoe Repair and buy a can of Neat's Foot Oil and rub it in. I did. I didn't just rub it in, I poured it in, from the inside. This worked: the combination of root-beer sugar and shoe oil made the leather darker, and there was an odd smell for a while, but the briefcase was fine, better than ever.

Then at my grandfather's funeral, one of my overly successful first cousins, all of whom went to Yale Medical

School and are full of shallow competencies—humph!—
said, "Here, I can put this in the back," and wrestled my
briefcase out of my hand and flipped it up and let it land
on the spare tire in the trunk of his rented car. He took
hold of both sides of it and pushed it back deeper into the
trunk, not noticing that there was a long bolt with a
rough edge projecting up from the bottom of the trunk,
onto which the spare tire was clamped, and that as he
pushed my briefcase across this bolt, it would scratch the
leather. This was no surface scratch—this was a deep,
straight gouge, a wound three eighths of an inch wide
that went all the way down one side, exposing the
leather's untanned layer. "Sorry," my cousin said. I took
my briefcase over to a stone parapet with a round
decorative cement globe in an urn and I bounced my fist
a few times against the urn's rough surface. When you
make a tight fist, your little-finger muscle, which runs
along the side of your hand, can bunch up and become
surprisingly springy, and if you time the fist-clenching
just right, you can use the sudden bunching of the muscle
to help send your fist back up in the air for the next
bounce. At the airport, my father looked at the briefcase
scratch, and he said, "I'd take it to Paul's Shoe Repair."

Paul sanded down the roughness of the scrape and dyed it a chocolate brown that wasn't a perfect match but was still very close. I used the briefcase for almost fifteen years, until finally both handles tore. Now it's in a box in the attic.

16

Good morning, it's 4:55 a.m.—Last night I went to bed at eight-thirty, and this morning I woke up having found a position in the bed that was one of the best bed positions I've ever been in. I must be getting better at sleeping. No part of me hurt or had stiffness; I was floating on a perfect angle of pillow and shoulder. I lay for fifteen minutes, thinking about the time long ago when I had a pet ant named Fidel, and then I heard Henry get up and pee and come into our room. His blankets had fallen off and he had gotten chilled. I lifted our covers so that he could get in, a small shivering boy with a very cold hand that he put on my shoulder. Claire was asleep. We three lay there for a while, Henry's nose against my back, until he warmed up and fell asleep; then I somehow managed to pour myself out of the bottom of the bed without waking either him or Claire, so that I could come down here and fire up the morning. I've just crumpled a colorful advertising supplement from Sears. Their slogan is "The Good Life at a Great Price." Every year on my birthday my mother would take me to buy a new pair of Sears work boots. They cost five dollars, and they would get very soft at the toe after a few months. Good boots they were, great boots, in fact. Boots wear out, but how many socket-wrench sets and circular saws can the world buy? I've lit the crumpled Sears circular. Blue ink sometimes burns bright green.

Home Depot is part of what is hurting Sears. Claire bought the unpainted doghouse that we use as a duck château at Home Depot. And this past weekend we went there to buy a mini-refrigerator, so that in the future, when houseguests come, they can have breakfast in their guest room, with their own butter and their own milk for their coffee and their own ultracool cantaloupe. While it's true that you can have very good conversations with houseguests in the morning, when everyone's hair is poking off in novel directions, it is also true that by the fourth day both guest and host, hoarse from forced cheer, will find that they may prefer to read the paper in their pajamas in different parts of the house. So we selected a mini-fridge. We stood in an aisle for a long time, waiting for a person to show up with an electric lift that he could use to pull down one of the several boxed fridges that were on an upper shelf. Finally the fridge-retriever arrived. He was a diminutive man who has advised us in the past on faucets. This Home Depot employs several very small people, if I'm not mistaken, and they're usually the most knowledgeable. Go right for the bearded dwarf with the tool belt if you want the best advice.

He rose up on the lift and, fifteen feet in the air, began wrestling with the mini-fridge. He whistled a Supertramp song loudly to convey that all was well. I didn't want to make him nervous by staring up at his struggles, so I turned and looked down the aisle. There was a lot going on. A couple was choosing between two pieces of white pipe, and farther down I saw a big woman in a sweater and leggings pointing up at something. She had a lot of hair. She mounted a moving metal stairway, one that has rollers on one end and rubber nubbins on the other, so that when you put your weight on them the nubbins act as brakes, and she unhooked a toilet seat from a display. She looked at it from several angles—a big angelic oval in the air above the heads of the ground-level shoppers—and then she handed it down to her husband. He held it for a while, nodding, then handed it back up to her. She rehung it on its hooks. By then our mini-fridge had landed.

So now there is quite a nice fridge in the guest room. Henry and Phoebe unpacked it, pulling off all the pieces of blue tape. It was similar to the unpacking of a new printer, which always has pieces of sticky-but-not-too-sticky tape holding the various movable elements in place.

And now Henry has appeared in the dawn-lit living room. I just asked him if he'd had a good sleep in our bed.

"Yes, I was quite warm," said Henry.

I asked him what made him wake up so early.

"Dad, you see, Mom said she was going to read me some more of the book we're reading, and I wondered if she was awake yet. And when I felt how warm it was, I snuggled in. I joined the party."

Henry puts the word Dad in practically every sentence he says to me. He seems to want to say the word Dad. Who is that Dad? I am.

"Dad, in only two years I'm going to be ten," he just

told me. He has tossed an egg carton onto the fire. There was a fall of large shaggy flakes yesterday; the wild grape at the end of our lawn and the tall pines across the valley are squirrel-tailed with snow. And now I can hear the crows, the birds that announce the end of my secret morning.

17

Good morning, it's 4:03 a.m., early, early, early. I did something new while the coffeemaker was snuffling and gasping: I washed a dish that I'd left last night in the sink to soak. Claire made a pathbreaking noodle casserole, which we ate three quarters of. One quarter is now socked away in the refrigerator. While I was filling up the carafe of the coffeemaker, it clinked against the glass casserole dish, and I thought what the hay. The dish was full of night-cooled water when I began. I put my hand in it. The suds were gone and the water was still—it was like taking an early-morning swim in the lake at camp, not that I ever did that. I could feel some hard places down on the bottom that would need scrubbing, and there were two dinner forks lurking below as well. I was glad to know about the forks, because if I had poured the water out without removing the forks I would have made a jangling that might have woken Henry. I got the water from the tap to a hot but not unbearable temperature and, having successfully felt for the rough-sided scrubber sponge and the container of dishwashing liquid, I squirted a big blind *C* over the bottom, where the baked-on cheese was. It was a silent *C:* as one gets better at squirting out dishwashing liquid one learns how to ease off at the end of a squirt so that one doesn't make an unpleasant floozling sound. And then I began to scrub, scooting over the smooth places and then ramming into the islands of resistance. Soon the baked-on atolls, softened overnight, began to give way: I pestered at the last one from the side for a while, smiling with the clenched-teeth smile of the joyful scrubber, and it was gone—no, there was still a tiny rough patch left behind to be dealt with, and then, oh sweet life, I could circle my sponge over the entire surface of the dish at the speed of the swirling water, frictionlessly, like a velodrome racer on a victory lap.

What a way to begin the day. You get to know a landscape by painting it; you get to know a dish by washing it—washing and rinsing it both, and there is a way of rinsing that I have developed over the years that uses less water, a low-flow method. Let some water run into the bottom and then work the dish to create a rotating wave that sloshes centrifugally up to the upper edge of the dish. Then dump that water and fill it again, and spin again. The idea is to remove all traces of soap, because soap tastes bad. And then—and this is a part that some people forget—you should turn the dish over and rinse the underside: for when a dish sits in the sink it can stamp itself onto bits of food and you don't want those bits going up on the shelf where they will harden. I got the dish settled in the drainer without making any loud clinks, and by that time my coffee was done.

What you do first thing can influence your whole day. If the first thing you do is stump to the computer in your pajamas to check your e-mail, blinking and plucking your proverbs, you're going to be in a hungry electronic funk all morning. So don't do it. If you read the paper first thing you're going to be full of puns and grievances—put that off. For a while I thought that the key to life was to read something from a book first thing. The idea was to reach down, even before I'd fully awakened, to the pile of books by the bed and haul one up and open it. This only works during the months of the year when you wake up in a world that is light enough to make out lines of print, but sometimes even when you open the book and can't quite read it in the grayness, or greyness, when you see the word that you know is a word hovering there in a granular dance of eye particles, and then you find that if you really stare at it you can read it, and the word is *almost,* the reading of that single word can be as good as reading a whole chapter under normal lighting conditions. Your fingertips are still puffy from sleep, and the corner of the book is the first sharp thing you feel, and you lift it open at random, not knowing what book your hands found, and there is that *almost* slowly coming into semi-focus in the gnat-swarms of dawnlight. It changes your whole day.

But now, see, now, I've gone beyond *almost.* Now I read nothing when I wake up, I just put on my bathrobe and come down here. Nothing has happened to me when I sit down in this chair, except that I've made coffee and rinsed an apple and, at least on this unusual morning, washed a casserole dish. I am the world, or perhaps the world is a black silk eye mask and I'm wearing it. This whole room warms up from the fire I've made: all the surfaces in the room, the picture frames, the Chinese teapot in the shape of a cauliflower, the glass coasters with Claire's grandmother's initials on them, the small wicker rocking chair that my father gave to Phoebe when she was four years old—all of it is warming up.

It occurs to me that I haven't described the fireplace. It isn't a Rumford fireplace. Rumford was a clever count who figured out, two hundred years ago, how to build fireplaces shallower, so that they would throw more heat into the room. This fireplace is almost a Rumford, but it is an earlier design. It is about a foot and a half deep, with diagonal brick sides. In the fireplace is a cast-iron grate; it is like a small porch or bandstand that holds the logs behind a low railing. There are decorative cast-iron urn shapes on each corner. What happens is that the iron gradually gets hotter, and the row of ornamental uprights in the balcony's railing radiates the heat out onto my feet. Because the grate holds the logs so steadily, I can put my feet an inch or so away from the flame in perfect comfort;

only when the fire has really begun burning hard do I sometimes have to move my chair back.

The first year we lived here we were spooked by the chimney experts and didn't have any fires. The man who sold us the house had stuffed quantities of pink insulation up all the openings. Once while I was unpacking things I heard an angry cheeping. I pulled on the insulation—a cloud of bird-dropping dust puffed out into the room. The cheeping got louder. I went to the bathroom, and when I returned I heard a nibbling sound along with an even louder cheeping, and I saw a bat crouched in a corner, wings half furled, furiously nibbling on a copy of *Harper's Magazine*. The bat was angry, baring its teeth like a dog, and the teeth were surprisingly fangy. There had been an article in the paper about rabies and bats; I thought there might be some possibility that this one was rabid. When I imprisoned it under an upside-down plastic trash basket, it began chattering furiously and gnawing at the plastic. I called animal control, which turned out to be a cherubic town policeman of maybe twenty-two and his niece of ten who sat in the patrol car. He trapped the bat in a lunchbox container with a screw-on lid. It was too expensive to test it for rabies, he said; he took a shovel out of his trunk and went off to a far corner of our yard, killed the bat and buried it there. We thanked him and he and his niece drove off. I felt that we'd done wrong. I certainly wouldn't have wanted to have been bitten by the bat, but now I think it probably wasn't rabid, just exhausted and mad after its tangle with the pink insulation.

Once we started using the fireplace, the bats moved to a comfortable spot in the eaves and had babies. Claire was looking out at the dusky sky one summer night from an upstairs window and saw many young ones, she said, black liquid drops, one after another, emerging from a shadowy hole.

Consider for a moment what the chimney sweeps had to do. I bet they ran into plenty of bats. I read about them one morning in a book of essays by Sydney Smith—I fished the book up first thing from the floor beside the bed and opened it to the table of contents, and there in the dimness was a title: "Chimney Sweepers." Sydney Smith had written the essay for the *Edinburgh Review* in 1819. The sweeps were boys of seven or eight or nine,

who would show up at the appointed house at three in the
morning and bang on the front door. The servants, still
asleep, wouldn't let them in, and so they would stand in
the cold, no socks, chilblains throbbing, waiting. They had
to be small in order to fit up the chimneys, of course, and
they worked all day in those tiny spaces, carrying the sack
of soot from one job to the next, and some got stuck and
died in the dark high corners, and before they became
hardened to the work their knees bled. One climbing
boy—so they were called—told an investigator for the
House of Lords that he climbed his first chimney because
his master told him that there was a plum pudding at the
top. A plum pudding is in effect a prune pudding, but that
wouldn't sound as good.

Now we think of Dick Van Dyke dancing his pipe-
stemmed, long-legged dance; real chimney sweeps
today are chatty men of thirty-five whose trucks are
expensively painted with Victorian lettering—they're
the sort of men who also like to dress up as clowns or
magicians for children's birthdays. But back in 1819,
it wasn't a good life, and I found when I read about
the climbing boys that I wanted to right the wrong

immediately—I wanted to mail letters urging legislative reform, as if the long-ago suffering could be fixed retroactively and all those lost lives redirected.

When we first moved here, we called a local chimney sweep—a software engineer who swept on weekends—who peered up into the brickwork and said that it was all rotten. No way could he sweep it until the chimney was rebuilt. A mason we talked to said the same thing: no fires until you do something radical. So we gave up on fires, and our first winter was very cold.

Then we invited Lucy, our neighbor, over for dinner. She scoffed at the mason and the chimney sweep. She said she used her chimneys every winter, even though they told her she mustn't. Our house had been here, she pointed out, for more than two hundred years, without once having burned, and the fireplaces had all been in use until very recently, and the two brothers who had owned the place hadn't installed woodstoves, which deposit creosote. It was unlikely that our chimneys would suddenly become terrible fire hazards; more likely that the experts were judging the old brick too harshly. Light a little fire and see if it draws, she said. Keep a blanket nearby—if you have a chimney fire, which probably won't happen, stuff the blanket up the chimney and it will cut off the air supply to the fire and put it out.

So we made a small test blaze, clutching an old blanket, and the fireplace worked perfectly. We tried all the fireplaces—they all worked. There was no problem. And the brickwork is in better shape than before because the fires have dried it out.

Some crows are outside; I can hear them. I'm going to take a shower and then feed the duck. She hears me coming and makes her small querying noises, but these days when I flip back the blanket and take away the screen, she drops to the ice and is still. I think it's because she has to wait until her eyes are adjusted to the daylight, and she wants to be motionless while the adjustment proceeds so as not to draw the attention of a predator. Yesterday, she riveted away at the food I sprinkled into the warm water, blowing snortingly through her beak-nostrils once or twice, and when I walked back to the porch she hurled herself into the air, honking loudly, and landed in a snow-pile, perfectly placed to hop into the porch. It was cold, so I let her come into the porch, and then into the house, where she followed me around, shaking her wings and tail. "Who do we have here?" said Claire at the top of the stairs. After the duck had a chance to get warm I carried her gently to the door and urged her out, feeling her small bones. She didn't want to go. She can't be an indoor duck because she leaves green duck artifacts everywhere in her excitement.

18

Good morning, it's 5:14 a.m., and it's cold, and the only creature stirring is the cat: he's just had an extended session in his litter box, scraping and scraping. He's got one of those litter boxes with the roof and the side hole: he climbs in and is able to turn smoothly around, and then he holds still with his head out the hole, slitting his eyes, until he is finished, and then the compulsive digging begins, the scrape of claws on grey plastic.

I woke up this morning and went into the bathroom and pulled down my pajama bottoms and silently peed, shivering, for a long time. I can accumulate a remarkable amount of urine. It's been almost fifteen years since I took to sitting down on the toilet to pee at night. Someone I worked with was complaining about her husband's bad aim in the bathroom, and someone else said her husband sat down and always had, and I was struck by this. Just because during the day you stand, does that mean that you must stand during the night as well? Of course not. There's no shame in sitting down, and here's what happens if you don't. In the middle of the night you don't want to turn on the light, because it hurts your eyes and makes it harder to go back to sleep, so you decide to go in the dark. You think you have a pretty good idea where the toilet bowl is. So you stand there in the dark, straining for cues and luminosities, saying to yourself that it's a very large bowl anyway and the chances are good that you'll hit the mark. And yet of course you're sleepy and you may have a slight nonsexual stiffening and you're clumsy. So you let some pee down into the darkness. You listen for the sound. Is it the sound of a fluid stream hitting water? That's good. Then you're fine. Is it, on the other hand, the sound of a coherent fluid stream hitting porcelain? That may be good or it may not be good, depending on whether you're hitting the porcelain of the actual inside of the bowl, around the water, or the porcelain on the edge. A doubt arises. Very probably it's the porcelain near the water. You'll know that it is near if you make a tiny left or right adjustment and hear the confirming sound of water. And you wonder, Which way do I adjust the aim? It seems like I might be aiming a little too much to the left. So you correct by directing the stream a little to the right, and the sound changes, and now you're in trouble, because it's the sound, you're pretty sure, of pee hitting rim and maybe even floor, so you quick jerk back to what you think is your original position. But it isn't the original position. You've lost your bearings now, you're wandering in an unknown forest, and you have a suspicion that maybe the stream has split into a V; when that happens, no amount of course correction will help. You clamp off the outflow and turn on the light to take stock. If you can't see anything on the floor, you're okay, but if there's an obvious small pool, then you have to get the undersink sponge going or use bunched-up toilet paper to dab it up, and the bending with the bunched toilet paper sends blood to the head, further waking you up. Now you're much more awake than you would have been had you turned on the light in the first place. Not all of the pee will be cleaned, either, because it is the middle of the night, and nobody cleans things up that well in the middle of the night. Eventually

over some weeks a faint smell will arise. That's why I
recommend sitting.

Also, if you sit your activity is silent; whereas if you
stand and you are lucky enough to hit water, the cat
wakes up at the noise and may pluck the bed.

Passing me by, passing me by. Life is. Five years ago I
planned to write a book for my son called *The Young
Sponge*. I was going to give it to him as a birthday present.
It was going to be the adventures of a cellulose kitchen
sponge that somehow in the manufacturing is made with
a bit of real sea sponge in it, giving it sentient powers.
It lives by the sink but it has yearnings for the deep
sea; it thirsts for the rocky crannies and the briny tang.
Then Nickelodeon came up with a show, and a pretty
good one, about a sponge. My idea was instantly dead: my
son would think I was merely copying a TV show.
Nickelodeon had acted, I had only planned to act.

Speaking of creative torpor, when my half-eaten apple
fell off the ashcan just now, it occurred to me that I don't
really know what the Ashcan school of art is. Yesterday
evening I felt the fireplace ash. It was cool, finally: deep-
red bits can stay alive for many hours. I shoveled some of
it into the tin container with a lid that was here when we

moved in—it must be the ashcan. The ash was a very light grey, almost white, and very fine—composed mostly, I imagine, of clay, which doesn't burn when paper burns. Henry, who was watching me, said: "Dad, think of all the stuff we've burned, and it all goes down to this much." It was only the third time I've shoveled out the fireplace. The ungraspableness of history, which can seem thrilling or frightening depending on your mood, can assert itself at any moment. I just found another small bedroll of lint in my automatic lint-accumulator and I tossed it into the fire: there was an almost imperceptible flare of differently colored fire—ah! *lint fire*—and it was gone. That is part of why I like looking at these burning logs: they seem like years of life to me. All the particulars are consumed and left as ash, but warm and life-giving as they burn. Meanwhile the duck is outside in the cold. She piles her excretions high in one corner, according to Claire, and she has a little declivity in the wood chips, where she fluffs up her feathers, but she's got to be cold out there. She will be so happy when things thaw and she has the mud along the creek to root around in. Yesterday I touched the feathers on the back of her neck: they don't look as if they would repel water quite as well as they did in the high summer, because she hasn't been able to swim in water. Yesterday, also, I heard her take off behind me and I turned to see an egg-shaped, cross-eyed form with windmilling arms flying towards me at head height. Often she changes course right at the very end of her flight, and this time she landed on an icy patch; her feet went back like a penguin's and she scooted a little. But she was unhurt.

I'm still fascinated by the ability of her feet to withstand cold. The cold must go right through that thick layer of skin into her leg bones. What she wants is more blueberries. Claire bought frozen blueberries for her and defrosted a cup of them in the microwave. You can feel strange worries about the nature of consciousness when you try to imagine what a duck is thinking about all night closed up in a doghouse with a bowl of slowly freezing water and some food pellets, with a screen door over the opening to keep out coyotes and a blanket over the screen door. Every so often, she roots a little in the shavings— looking for what? She wants grubs and worms, but there aren't any now, too cold. Why does she exist? We as a family exist to be nice to the duck, and the duck exists to puzzle us. Who would have known that ducks make desperate sounds, trembly murmuring squeals, when you hold out a handful of pellets for them? Who would have known that she prefers to be fed by hand than to have the food in her bowl? What she likes best is to have you hold out to her a handful of pellets over the warm water. That way when she jabs at them with her beak, some fall into the water, and she can rap away at them under the water, snuffling through her beak-nostrils, and then come back up and get some dry pellets again, up and down.

She seems less interested in the cat's anus: he keeps a distance and has returned to his primary mission, asserting the rights of private property against neighborhood coon cats.

I just laid a Quaker Oats container on the fire, which had burned down to a dim red glow. The cylinder flamed, blindingly, and the Quaker in the black hat, smiling, was engulfed. What is left now looks like some war-blackened martello tower on a distant coast. I looked over to the window to see if there was any light yet outside, but the curtains were drawn: Claire sometimes closes them at night because they are, she's right, a kind of insulation. But I think I'll pull one of them open now so that I can see the hints of light outside as I work.

"It's completely dark," I whispered when I pulled back the curtains. The glass, though, had a good smell of summer-afternoon dust in it.

19

Good morning, it's 5:44 a.m., and I'm up late again, but I've got four big old logs on the fire, each with a layer of burn-scabs from yesterday evening that break off when I rearrange them. The coffee is extra strong this morning; I poured in some from the less good bag so that we wouldn't run out of our reserves in the good bag. Phoebe is disappointed in herself because she didn't say interesting things when a restaurateur came to dinner last night. She appeared, dressed with great care in a T-shirt with tiny sleeves, her bangs perfect in a fourteen-year-old way, in the living room, and listened while the restaurateur told Claire about his drive through Nova Scotia, and I carved off bits of nutty cheese log and scraped them onto crackers. Finally, the restaurateur asked Phoebe how her school was. Phoebe described her science project, in which she baked three small cakes, each made with a different brand of baking soda, to see which one would rise more. "Hm," said the restaurateur. Phoebe went quiet again. Afterward she said, "I wanted to ask him how you get to be a chef and instead I just sat there."

"You told him about your baking-soda project."

"I'm a boring person," she said.

I told her that she wasn't a boring person, and she insisted that she was, and I countered that she wasn't, and then we got onto the subject of the unnecessary repaving of Calkins Road, which took us to the subject of war crimes, and that we discussed till ten-fifteen, which is why I got up late.

I'm glad there are fifty-two weeks in the year—it seems like the right number, and there is the interesting congruity with a deck of cards. But there really should be more than twelve months. January is one of my favorites, and we're getting towards the end of it. My children are practically grown, and my beard—I'm not at all content with my beard. Fortunately February is a pretty good month, too, so I'll still be okay. They're all pretty good months, actually, it's just that there aren't enough of them. On New Year's morning this year Claire got us to drive to the ocean to watch the sun rise. That outing was what made me suddenly understand that I needed to start reading Robert Service again and getting up early—that New Year's outing combined with the time a few months ago when I took the night sleeper car from Washington to Boston and woke up in my bunk and pulled the curtain to look out the window and saw that we were in the station in New York City, and I realized that I was passing through a very important center of commerce without seeing a single street and that something similar was happening in my life.

On New Year's morning we packed two thermoses, one of hot chocolate and one of coffee, and we drove for half an hour, the four of us, to the little parking lot at the beach. There was a bitter wind that made our pants flap, but several people were there with their dogs, looking out at the places on the horizon where they expected the sun to rise. Some seemed to know where it would come up and some didn't; one old couple, bundled and hooded in matching orange puffy coats, stood still, halfway down to the water, mitten in mitten. I figured that they would know where the sun would appear and, yes, they did. It underwent some waistline contortions, as rising suns so often do, narrowing first and then oozing out as if from a puncture in the seam of the horizon, and then the sky around the puncture point became inconceivably blue.

That was this year. Last year for New Year's I decided that I would shave off my beard because there was too much white in it. I bought an electric trimmer, and I began plowing off chunks of coarse fur. Henry watched with interest, but Phoebe became unexpectedly upset. She said that my personality had to have a beard. I must stop immediately, she said. I said I was tired of looking in the mirror at a prematurely white-bearded person—that I had no respect or affection for badger-people in their forties. If, after I finished buzzing it off, I didn't like the results, then I would just regrow it. When I was halfway through, Henry said, "Dad, I think it looks interesting but you need to work some on the other side." Claire said to Phoebe, "He's just seeing how it looks." But I could see that when she, Claire, saw me in the mirror she was a little startled.

You see, Claire had never seen me beardless. I've had one since I was eighteen, and in years past I've been more than a little proud of its curly density and its russet highlights. By the way, you can trim a beard, I've found, using a double-bladed disposable razor: you "shave" over the beard's shape as if it were your jaw and chin. I originally grew the beard because I thought I had a thin weak face, which I did, but over the years, without my knowledge or consent, it had changed into a plump weak face. The mouth was the main problem: I had always thought that I had a generous ho-ho-ho sort of mouth, the mouth of a backslapping mountain man, quick with a knock-knock joke or a kindly word, but it turned out, when put in the context of my upper lip, that my mouth was pursed and almost parsonly. That evening Claire kept getting caught by surprise by my face. "I can hear your voice in the room," she said, "but when I look up, you're not there," she said. I buried my head in her bathrobe so that she wouldn't see me; I was reminded of a time in seventh grade when someone kicked me during a soccer game and I spent the day with a puffed lip and thick twists of toilet paper projecting from both nostrils. Every time the teacher looked in my direction he laughed, and then he apologized for laughing, saying that he just couldn't help it.

It was a good experiment, Claire said, worth trying, but she liked my beard and wanted it back. I began regrowing it immediately.

20

Good morning, it's 4:39 a.m. and I just watched a cocktail napkin burn. After its period of flaming was past, there was a long time during which tiny yellow taxicabs did hairpin turns around the mountain passes, tunneling deeper and deeper into the ashen blackness. I've torn off some pages of a course catalog for a local community college and I've rolled them up and pushed them into the hot places. Because I started late yesterday, I was in a rush to be sitting here in front of the fire by five a.m. sharp, and that is probably why I stepped on Henry's airplane in the dining room. Out of a paper-towel tube, an electric motor, a battery holder, a light switch, and a great deal of masking tape, Henry made an airplane. He was sure that it would fly, even though Claire and I both gently, in different ways, observed that though it was beautiful it was heavy. Henry cut out larger and larger propellers from the lid of a shoebox, and he tried to tape on a second battery pack, and he and I went outside just before dinner and climbed the snowplow mound. He turned on the propeller and flung his machine out into the twilight. It landed heavily, but it seemed to be not too badly damaged. We came back inside. Phoebe and Claire were watching an episode of *Gomer Pyle*. I showed Henry how to make a paper airplane. I'd showed him once a few years ago, but he'd forgotten, and I'd almost forgotten myself. The moves came back to me, though, as I talked my way through them, and as the triangles narrowed into swept-back wings Henry began to make a purring, half-laughing sound of enlightenment that I thought he had stopped making forever.

So swerving to avoid the dining-room chair this morning, I stepped on the battery-powered airplane. I felt it for breakage, but I think it's all right——Henry had fortified it with more masking tape after its snow crash. Then, hurrying to be in here by five——not running but moving with a distinct sense of hurry——I felt a need to let out some private gas before I sat down, and because I didn't want to make any noise I paused for a moment and pulled on one side of my bottom—*backside* perhaps is a more delicate term—to allow the release to proceed without fanfare. Then I came in here and set up.

I wish I were a better photographer. Many family moments are going by and I'm missing most of them. At least I got a few shots last month when we had that very soft white snowfall that ticked against the window all night. It was an unusual snow, almost like Styrofoam in its consistency in some of the deep places, and when you dug in it, the light that it let through was an interesting sapphire blue—perhaps different prevailing temperatures during snowflake-growth result in a different shape of crystal, which absorbs and allows passage to different wavelengths of light. That Saturday Henry and I dug a tunnel through the snowplow pile. The duck became interested in our project—companionably she climbed to the top, beaking around in it for bits of frozen mud. When both of her feet got cold at the same time she sat down in the snow for a while to warm them. Once or twice she levitated, flapping hard. She didn't much want to walk through the tunnel, and we didn't make her.

Towards the end of the tunneling I got the camera

and took two pictures of Henry looking out, with his hood on and his nose red from cold. Then I was out of film. My pictures used to be better than they are now. About ten years ago I bought a Fuji camera that took fantastic pictures. It was a simple point-and-shoot machine, but the lens was good. Then a few years ago, I was packing our car for a trip. I was holding several things in my left hand—the Fuji by its strap, my battered briefcase, and a shopping bag full of presents—and I was concentrating on my right hand, in which I was holding a suitcase and a coat, but also reaching through the handle of the suitcase to open the back hatch of the car. As I put the things in the car, my overspecialized fingers, forgetting that some of them were doing double duty, relaxed their hold on the camera strap when they released the handle of the shopping bag, so that the camera fell, not in a broken, lurched-after tumble, but straight down, freely released, onto the street. It worked after that for a while, but it rattled in a very un-Japanese sort of way, and finally it stopped focusing. The camera store said they couldn't repair it, so I bought a new camera, more expensive, waterproof, to replace it, but the pictures it takes are not as good, or else my skill has declined.

These unintentional droppings of held objects have occurred to me at least twenty times in my life. Trouble ensues, for instance, when I have a heavy load from the dry cleaners hanging on coat hangers in a hand that is also holding something else. You can hook a lot of coat hangers onto two fingers, but they pull back the fingers and dig into the skin of the inside fingerjoints, and those heavy coat-hanger sensations are powerful enough to distract from the sensation of whatever other thing those fingers may be responsible for—the mail, say, which falls in the slush. I'm prone to other absentminded acts as well. I once pulled a bag of garbage from the kitchen can, tied it, and hung it on a hook in the hall closet. "Did you just hang up that bag of garbage in the closet?" Claire asked me. "I believe I did," I said, thinking back. Another time I was standing in a kitchen talking to my mother-in-law and drinking a cup of tea. Admiring the teacup, I asked her whether it was Hollerbee china, knowing that she had gone to the Hollerbee outlet with Claire several times and bought things. My mother-in-law said she wasn't sure where it came from. I turned it over to see if it had the Hollerbee logo on the underside, and it did. But I'd forgotten that there was tea in the cup.

I suppose if I taught at a college I would gradually drift into the role of the absent-minded professor. One of Claire's history teachers in college showed up late to class one morning with his wife's bra clinging to the back of his sweater. Another morning, lighting a pipe near a longhaired student, he gestured with a match. A smell of hot hair filled the room; the professor, not noticing, continued his lecture.

Once I lost a key. I spent a day looking for it before I gave up; a week later Claire found it frozen to the bottom of a piece of raw meat that she took out of the freezer. I don't know how it got there.

21

Good morning, it's 5:25 a.m., and last night was less good from the point of view of sleep. I had to pull out some of my old suicide fantasies—like the one where I'm the only passenger on a roller coaster that is fitted out with a horizontal blade at the top of one of its turns. I swoop up towards the high turn and the switchblade flips out into my path, chopping off my head. Released from my body, I tumble placidly through space, closing my eyes. Another one I tried was my self-filling grave idea, a mainstay in high school. If you kill yourself, you are being inconsiderate, because others must deal with the distasteful mess of your corpse. The self-filling grave solved that. You dig for a long time, mounding all the dirt on a sheet of plywood by the hole, and when you've gotten the grave just the way you want it, with the roots neatly trimmed off and a layer of soft, cool, fertile dirt in the bottom and no stones, you put a chair in the grave—not one of any value—and you clamp a revolver to the back of the chair pointing diagonally out and fitted with a remote-control trigger; and then you arrange a complicated system of pulleys and weights so that when you shoot yourself fatally and fall into the soft cool fertile earth, your fall will cross a tripwire that pulls away a prop and allows the load of dirt to slide in after you. The dumping of the dirt in turn triggers the flapping down of a large piece of biodegradable two-ply fabric, between the layers of which you have sprinkled grass seed, wildflower seed, and weed seed, in the proper pro-portions. After a few months, if all goes well, nobody will know where you are buried—except that the tilted sheet of plywood attached to the system of ropes and counterweights may occasion curiosity. I never end up actually dead in these fantasies. I can't die: I have to be able to check whether, for example, the proportion of wildflowers to grass seed is too rich and must be adjusted down.

From college I once sent my grandmother what I

thought was a good letter. She sent a chatty letter back, but at the top there was an arrow pointing to the date, and she had written, in larger handwriting, "By the by, always *date* your letters." Her flaw-finding note hurt my feelings, but she was right, and from that moment on I became extremely date conscious. I date every piece of children's art that we keep (on the back, in tiny lettering), and I made sure that the Fuji camera had a "date-back" feature: it burned the date, year first, in orange fiery letters on the lower right-hand side of every picture.

In the last letter my grandmother wrote us, when she asked for another picture of Phoebe to brighten the front of her refrigerator, she didn't date the letter. No date anywhere. I had to note it on the letter myself, referring to the canceled stamp. I should have known then that she was letting go.

I took the plane down the day after she'd broken her back. My grandfather was downstairs playing his Chopin prelude. I called an ambulance; she cried out with a terrible pain-cry when they moved her a certain way on the stretcher, which they had trouble maneuvering around the hallway to her room. But she got better. She didn't believe in the dishwasher; she stored cans of soup in its top rack. While she was in the hospital, I taught my grandfather how to heat up a can of tomato soup, and how to put a load of laundry in the washing machine.

For years she'd written (not just typed, but written) all of his scientific correspondence, and yet he insisted on moving to new universities and research centers, where he would attempt to carry on. When my grandmother was angriest at him—over the oblivious playing of the Chopin while her back was broken—she said to me in a whisper that the three fungal diseases he was known for were partly hand-me-downs from one of his teachers at Yale. What really bothered her was his autobiography. He had given it to her to edit. In the third chapter, he wrote that he proposed to her one afternoon, and then hurried back to his microscope to examine some interesting slides of coccidioidomycosis, prepared with a new kind of stain—and that was the last mention of her. "He is, I think, an affectionate person," she said, "but he takes after his mother." His mother was a self-absorbed and difficult birdwatcher who moved in soon after my grandparents were married and then grew vague and quarrelsome. My grandmother said, "There was one time, Emmett, when I was out for a drive, just on some errand, and there was a steep slope on one side of the road, and it was everything I could do to keep myself from driving right off the edge." I said that I was very sorry it had been so difficult. "I'm really letting my hair down," she said. I'd never heard that idiom before. Her hair was white with many gentle curls; it could not be let down.

She loved her four children, though, and was good to them, and I do believe that it made her happy to be a grandmother. Also she liked that she knew where everything was in her house, and that she could list all the books of the Old Testament at high speed. She gave Claire a bag of rags, for polishing things, when we were engaged; one of her aunts had given her a bag of rags and she'd much appreciated it. Always date your letters, she taught me. Thank goodness for that Fuji camera.

22

Good morning, it's 5:33 a.m. and I'm feeling better about my beard. Yesterday I was going through a box of clothes and I found a dark blue sweater that I'd forgotten about. It has a silvery white pattern of small shapes in it, and these bring out the silver in my beard or at least make it look less unintentional.

We've run out of apples, so I've brought in a pear. I've held it up to the fire to read the label, which says "#4418 Forelle," and then, around that, in capitals in a green border, RIPE WHEN YIELDS TO GENTLE PRESSURE. I woke up at 5:15, shivering. I could feel each shiver system with more detail, more precision, than normal. It began in my torso and then rose, vibrating, up my spine until I could feel the muscles in the back of my neck participating, and then it was gone. The duck sometimes shivers. I was glad to learn when I was a child that shivering serves a useful purpose, and is not simply a signal of cryothermic distress, although it clearly is a sign of that as well, since it feels bad. You know that if you're shivering you must go inside or put on something warmer and you want to do that because the sensation of the shivering is unpleasant. But for some animals, who don't have any warm places to go to, the shivering may be a neutral or even a pleasurable sensation, a way of passing the time.

I've thrown my eaten pear into the fire. Phoebe cleaned her room yesterday and found two lost pairs of scissors there, one of which I am going to use to clip my mustache so that when I go out for lunch today I won't get salad dressing on it and have to use my tongue to draw some of the mustache into my mouth and suck the lunch off. My beard has gotten long enough that it can become sleep-squashed on one side and flared-out on the other. Sometimes on the weekend I don't take a shower until late in the afternoon, and then if I go to the store I have to fluff my beard into symmetry in the rearview mirror.

People seldom give me strange looks, though, so I must not seem too eccentric.

My pear had bird's-egg specklings of a delicacy I'd never before seen on a pear, and seldom on a bird's egg, either. It wasn't quite ripe, though; it didn't have that superb grittiness of skin, when the flesh dissolves and the disintegrating skin grinds against your molars. Apple skin must be chewed heavily and steadily, and even so its slick, sharp-cornered surfaces survive a lot of molaring. But eating a ripe pear is similar to cutting a piece of paper with a pair of scissors: you feel the grit of the cut paper transmitted back through the blades to your fingers, you can sense that fulcrumed point of sharp intersection. Scissors are one of the many products that have gotten better in my lifetime. They used to become loose and wobbly at the hinge, and when they wobbled they would fold the paper between the blades instead of cutting it. But if you pushed the thumb-handle in the opposite direction to the larger loop of the finger-handle as you closed the two loops, even loose blades could be made to cut fairly well.

When I was a kid nobody cut (as many do now)

wrapping paper by steering the scissors through the paper without moving the blades—that was a later discovery, or else it depended on a certain kind of soft wrapping paper or a certain level of scissor sharpness. I bought the scissors in San Diego—they are made in China, and they have red plastic handles.

I don't feel so good.

Another machine we had in San Diego was a hose organizer—a machine you cranked, winding the hose up like a piece of thread. There was a hose-guide that slid so that you could coil the hose evenly on its spool. When we moved away, we gave the hose organizer to our next-door neighbors; they seemed to want it. When you coil a hose manually after watering with it you have to slide the whole thing through your left hand, which guides it into a series of lassoing circles by the faucet. The hose is wet when you wind it, so that as you drag it back it collects bits of mulchy things, which then get on your hands, and snail slime, whereas if you have a hose organizer you feel like a crew member on a merchant vessel, hoisting the anchor or squaring the mainsail.

Good morning, it's 5:20 a.m.—I thought the shivering was just from cold, but yesterday at work I began to have feverish feelings, and now I'm weak and the smell of the flaring match makes me feel very ill. I've tasted an apple from a brand-new bag of apples, but what I want to do is lie down on the floor. The blizzard yesterday was lost on me, and I spent all night with little delusional half-thoughts.

I'm going to lie down on the floor now, where it's cool.

Good morning, it's 6:30 a.m.—All yesterday I could feel the veins in my temples feeding the headache. In the morning, I was talking to Claire when I coughed abruptly and got up to go to the bathroom and then, thinking that this couldn't possibly be happening, I vomited a huge splash of water, Tylenol, and apple bits onto the bathroom floor before I made it to the toilet. I felt like a wind sock on a windless day. After the violence of the throwing up was over, and I had gotten my nosebleed under control, I asked Claire to bring a mop and I asked Henry to bring a roll of paper towels, and in the surge of good feeling that follows hours of nausea, I cleaned everything up. I threw out my socks; they had holes in the heels anyway. Then I went back to bed and slept, and when I woke I had a killer headache which lasted all day. But Claire brought me up tonic water and saltine crackers at one point, and though I threw up one more time I think that phase is over. I have something going on deep in my chest. Juliet, the woman next door who runs the day-care center, has been sick with pneumonia; she quite cheerfully told Claire her medieval symptoms at the bus stop and then Claire told them to me.

By feeding it some of an old telephone book, and a whole six-pack soft-drink holder, and an empty baking-soda box, I've finally gotten the fire to start. I don't know how long I'll be able to sit here, but I do feel fortunate to be able to do it at all. I have a glass of tonic water and five saltines on the ashcan next to my leg. Oh, the little sparkles of salt on the crackers, and the clear sweetness of the tonic water. We didn't have any ginger ale, but tonic water will do.

I knew I had a fever yesterday, but at first I had no desire to use a thermometer. You just know——with your children, too. Just touch them on their backs, below their necks, and if it's very warm there, then, yes, they have a fever. The moon is out on the prowl this morning. I slept for fifteen minutes at a time all day, dream-chewing on gristly ground-up pieces of thought, turning on one side and then the other, lifting the covers with my hand so that my knees could pass without sending the covers off the bed. Maybe I should go back to bed now. My head swivels listlessly, like a brussels sprout in boiling water, and yet all I've got is the flu. I think I'll have another cracker.

Yesterday towards evening I started to feel better and I decided that I would in fact like to know my temperature. If I didn't know, I wouldn't be giving my sickness its fair due, since the only real achievement of a sickness is the creation of a fever. The rest is dross. I found the thermometer and got back in bed, leaning against the pillows, and slid the glass swizzle-stick down into the fleshly church basement below my tongue, on the right side of that fin of stretchable tissue that goes down the middle. The cool glass almost had a flavor, but didn't; maybe it was the flavor of sitting at a lunch counter in the afternoon, looking out the window. My bottom jaw came forward a bit so that I could gently cradle the instrument with my teeth, and I held my lips pursed, waiting for the mercury to warm itself in my deepest salival catch basins; and as I waited I looked around the room, grazing my fingernails on what proved to be an unusually interesting stretch of wall. Every once in a while the thermometer would slip out a little ways and I would frown and clamp it firmly with my teeth and then chimp it back into place with my lips. Finally it was time to see what my temperature was. I held the glass very close to my eyes and turned it. At first I saw liquidly swollen numbers dancing and drinking sherry on the far side of the triangle, and then, turning more, these hove around and became precise and fringed with well-tended gradation lines, and behind them flashed the infinitely thin silver band, the soul of the body's temperature, stopped at a little under 101 degrees. I sank back with some relief: I did in fact have a fever. "My fever is a hundred and one!" I called out to whoever could hear.

"Very sorry to hear that, Dad!" Phoebe called from her room. She was writing a one-page paper on Voltaire.

I thought of those five-hundred-pound people in the tabloids who can't leave their beds. Then I remembered a picture of a woman with a growth-hormone disease. She is growing and growing without stop. Some years ago, she pleaded for Michael Jackson to send her money, and he had, but now who knows? He has his own deformities to contend with.

25

Good morning, 3:49 a.m. and I'm behaving as if everything's normal. When my apple fell off the ashcan, again, it made a low ominous sound as it rolled across the floor, and I remembered a review I read as a child of a Roman Polanski movie in which someone's head is chopped off and bounces down the steps. This room is not level or plumb. There is a large hump in the floor in one corner: over the years the floorboards have simply twisted and bent to fit whatever stresses were being imposed on them. I've been awake for an hour and a half, flipping through worry's Rolodex. I'm drinking coffee, oddly enough, and there lies a tale. Claire, knowing that I was determined to get up as usual this morning, very kindly set up the coffeemaker before she went to bed. I, sleepily, swiveled open the filter basket and saw in the dimness that it wasn't empty and dumped it out; but the filter seemed to fall into the garbage too easily. Only when I poured water into the tank of the coffeemaker and there was an answering sound of water already there did I realize that I'd just thrown out fresh coffee.

I spent almost all yesterday morning in bed dozing, and finally got into work around one. Now my coccyx hurts—the chest infection has descended to my tailbone, or has awakened an old wound. Last year I fell on my tailbone while getting into the car. Tears sprung, pain speared. And that event was an awakening of a very old injury, when once in fifth grade I went sledding down a steep hill. I had a long ride, without incident, and then came to what looked like an insignificant little drop-off from a snow-pile into a snow-covered school parking lot. That little drop landed me right on my tailbone. I hurt there for months afterward. I think I may have broken something, but tailbones are like toes, vestiges of tree-dwelling primates. You don't really need to worry too much about whether they're broken or just bruised.

To cool down just now I walked to the dining room, and I almost sat down on the two stairs between the dining room and the kitchen and rested, but instead I walked into the kitchen and had a glass of water. The moon is everywhere—it's impossible to say what color it is—I thought there was new snow but it was just moon.

Several years ago I decided that I would make a collection of paper-towel designs. Hundreds of patterns were coming and going, offered by the paper-towel makers, and unlike wallpaper patterns nobody was interested in studying them as indicia of American taste. Do you remember when suddenly one of the manufacturers began printing in four colors? I think it was 1996. I had in mind a big folio, with a pane of a towel on each page, and a label of what it was, who had made it, the date, notes, etc. I saved maybe eight paper-towel samples and then abandoned the project: I lack the acquisitive methodicalness that you need to create a really great paper-towel collection. And the main point is that the designs that I would want to have collected, the ones at the top of my want list, are the ones from my own childhood and my early marriage. The designs now are perfectly fine, but the designs then—the sampler-inspired patterns and the alternating pepper grinders and carrots—held an allegorical fascination. Of course there was more excitement over paper towels then—the vast advertising budget for Bounty, the Quicker Picker-Upper, made it so. A big change in paper towels since the advent of bulk-purchase stores has been the variation in frame size. The old rolls had a perfectly consistent size across all brands, which was very helpful because then you got so that you could tear off a frame without thinking. Then one manufacturer made much longer towel frames, for unknown reasons—perhaps to get us to use them up faster—and I was forever yanking the roll off of its holder, pulling in the wrong place. The roll that I used today has excessively short frames—good, though, because you use less per yank. But consistency has gone all to hell.

If you put your face very close to the window, you sense through the glass the coldness outside. I went upstairs to go to the bathroom and was amazed by how magnificently cool our bedroom was. Claire got up to pee and she said, sleepily, "I set up the coffee for you."

"I know, I'm terribly sorry."

"You threw it out."

"I did, I'm sorry."

"We'll just have to order Chinese," she murmured, falling asleep.

I asked her if she had a need for anything I might have stowed away in my pajamas.

"All set for the moment, thanks," she said.

I keep thinking of a knee operation I had years ago, when I watched the arthroscopic probe on a small screen and saw my kneecap from underneath, like an ice floe from the perspective of a deep-diving seal, with a few bubbles that looked like air but were, said the surgeon, bubbles of fat. He sewed up my torn meniscus and I was better, having read eight murder mysteries, none of which I can remember. No, I can remember one. There was a Perry Mason novel, by Erle Stanley Gardner, in which a character in a ship goes up on deck because he wants "a lungful of storm." That's what I want—a lungful of storm.

26

Good morning, it's 4:21 a.m. and the birch bark is burning well. I can pick up a pair of underwear with my toes. There are two ways to do this. Most people would grab a bunch of fabric by using all of their short, stubby, "normal" toes to clamp it against the ball of their foot and lift it, but because of my unusual middle toes, which are long and aquiline—distinguished—I can lift up the underwear by scissoring my middle toe and my big toe together onto the waistband: then I lift the underpants and hand them off to my hand and flip them towards the dirty-clothes bin. By then I'm ready to fall over, but I catch myself by planting my underpant-grasping foot back down on the floor. If you throw underpants in a particular way, the waistband assumes its full circular shape in the air, slowly rotating, on its way towards the dirty clothes.

Yesterday, having thus dealt with my underclothing, I had my shower, which was uneventful but for a moment near the middle. I was replacing the soap in the rubber-covered wire soap holder that hangs over the showerhead. It's a helpful holder because the soap dries out between mornings, whereas soap that sits in the corner of the shower or in a ridged cubby or a built-in ledge does not. I use Basis soap because it has no brain-shriveling perfumes. It is filled with very dense heavy soap material: it's harder and heavier than, say, Ivory soap. And it is a beautiful smooth oval shape, an egglike shape almost. But it's as heavy as a paperweight, as hard as travertine when dry or newly wetted, and extremely slippery. More than once I have lost control of a bar of this soap. And yesterday when I dropped it I noticed that as soon as the soap squirted out of my fingers, my toes lifted, arching up from the tub as high as they could go, while the rest of my feet stayed where they were. Both sets of toes did this immediately, as soon as the soap left my grip. My toes had evidently learned something in life, ever since the chilblains that I got one winter. What they have learned is that if they are touching the floor of the tub and a bar of soap drops on them, it is going to hurt a lot; however if the toes are lifted up half an inch in the air, much of the energy of the collision will be absorbed as the egg of soap forces the tightly stretched toe-tendons to elongate, and the impact on chilblains or healing toe-bones won't be nearly as painful. They learned this by trial and error, over many years, all by themselves, and now each time I fumble a bar of soap they arch up, on alert, braced for possible impact. My eyes are closed during all this, so I have no idea where the soap is falling; after it hits the tub, making a bowling-alley sound, they relax.

One of my middle toes has, as my coccyx does, an Old Injury. At seventeen, in the summer, I was the night cook at a busy place called Benny's: I cleaned the kitchen after closing, wiping down all the surfaces, pouring bleach on the cutting boards and draining the fryers and, last of all, mopping the floor. At first the cleaning took me until four in the morning, and my ankles swelled from standing for twelve hours; later I got faster, and I began cleaning our own home kitchen for pleasure, shaking out the toaster and going in under the burners on the stove. I was promoted to night cook when the head cook walked out on beer-batter-fish Friday, our biggest night. The manager and the assistant manager took up stations at the fryers—I specialized in onion rings. Too forcefully I pulled out a metal drawer filled with half-gallon cartons of semi-frozen clams; the drawer came out and fell on my toe. The pain was tremendous. I hum-whispered a long quavery moan to myself, but the show had to go on— I began making the icy clams dance around in the breadcrumbs.

Before he quit, the head cook passed on two pieces of information that I haven't forgotten. The first was in response to my insistence that the kitchen had to be clean. "It's all food anyway," he said. The second came when I forgot that an order was for a cheeseburger and not a hamburger. "Watch," the cook said. He took a square of American cheese and dipped it for a moment in the hot water in the steam table. The cheese melted a little and, when flopped down on the burger, looked deliciously semi-molten. The steam-table water was not clean, however; I almost dipped a piece of cheese into it myself but didn't.

I liked a waitress with a wide pretty face and a mouth whose many teeth forced her to smile generously. We took a break together once; she said that she wanted to be a poet. Her favorite poet was Rod McKuen, she said.

Benny's Restaurant is gone now: now there is a drugstore on that corner with fake dormer windows in its roof that are lit from inside by recessed fluorescence to create the impression that there are cozy upstairs bedrooms behind them. Few now can testify, as I can, to the wondrously bad smell that came from the Benny's Dumpster out back. What a marvelous, piercingly awful smell it had. People sometimes wanted breakfast very late at night, and I could never master over-easy eggs; they often broke when I flipped them, and I tried to hide the broken one with a piece of careless toast. I got compliments on my onion rings, though.

27

Good morning, it's 5:42 a.m.—I thought I was being clever last night by setting the fire up with paper, cardboard, and logs, so that I could just strike a match and begin this morning. Deep in the coals, however, the heat had persisted, and it lit my preset fire prematurely, sometime in the middle of the night, so that by the time I arrived fifteen minutes ago, the logs had coaled down to an orange skeleton crew. *Start building.* On *Jeopardy,* when someone turns out not to be as smart as he thought, and he bets everything and loses, and goes down to nothing while the others are in the thousands, Alex Trebek, the master of ceremonies, will say to him, "Start building."

I have a very stuffed nose now, and when I sleep my teeth dry out because I breathe through my mouth, and then my lips stick to them as if to pieces of sunbaked slate, and that fixed grimace wakes me up, and then comes that good moment when you push your lips out and down so that the teeth remoisten again. First they resist, and then the sliding resumes all at once, and you baste your teeth and get your tongue, which has also suffered an hour of desiccating privations, moving again. Oh, I am happy being up like this. Who would have known that I am and maybe always have secretly been an early-morning man? I would not have known it. Claire took us to see the sunrise on New Year's morning, and that has changed me. I used to be amused by those men who get to work at six-thirty, "bright and early"—but they're right: you want to be doing things when the world is still quiet; the quietness and uncrowdedness is your fuel. Except for me the phrase would be "dark and early."

While on the subject of fuel—I think I know why I'm feeling especially lucky this morning. It's because yesterday I hit sixteen dollars exactly when I filled the car with gas. I unscrewed the cap and put it on the roof of the car, and I selected the fuel grade, regular, and I started pumping. The metal of the pump was very cold on the finger-bones; the hose jumped a little when the gas started flowing through. I looked up from my gassing crouch and stared at the electronic numbers on the pump, trying to take in the movements of the rushing cents' column, which go by so fast that you end up only being able to make sense of the pieces of the LED numbers that each numeral has in common: the 4, the 5, and the 6, for instance, all have a middle horizontal stick, but the stick winks off for the 7, and then it comes back on for the 8 and 9, then off for the 0 and the 1; and there are other rhythms as well, so that each ten-cent cycle has a good deal of blinking syncopational activity. But don't let yourself get hooked on studying that. After five dollars' worth goes by you have to steel yourself to ignore the winks in the cents column and concentrate on the basic thumping beat of the dimes column. Get that rhythm in your head and then start tapping your foot steadily to that beat so that you become an automaton of steady flow—30, 40, 50, 60, 70. Keep counting up past ten dollars, and eleven, and twelve, watch those mystic dollars change, and don't release the handle, don't slow the flow, run the gas full throttle, counting and chanting and tapping the numbers like the monster of exactitude you are, and then get ready to release all at once, coonk. Yesterday I originally shot for fourteen dollars, and then when I got close to fourteen, I felt as if I was good for fifteen, and then when I came up on fifteen I said to myself, "Go for sixteen, you sick bastard," and I clenched my teeth and stared and counted six, seven, eight, nine, and *off*. Often I'm disappointed: the number will stop at \$16.01 or even \$16.02—seldom below. But no, yesterday the numbers stopped dead on \$16.00 and I said, "Bingo, baby." When you hit it on the money, a good thing will happen to you that day. In my case the good thing was that when I went in to pay for the gas I noticed a box of donuts on a convenient donut display right by the register. Three kinds of donut—cinnamon, plain, and white powder that makes you cough—were all in the same box, all showing through the plastic window like the mailing address to a world in which everyone spoke with his mouth full. I bought them, even though it meant I couldn't just hand over a twenty-dollar bill, and when

I showed up at home holding the box over my head as I crunched through the snow to the porch, my son opened the door and said, "Donuts! Bingo, baby." I used to go for the cinnamon-powdered ones, but now I find that old-fashioned donuts have a slightly bitter astringency that leaves your teeth feeling cleaner after you've eaten one, as I just have.

28

Good morning, it's 4:32 a.m. and there's that train whistle, a-tootin' in the night. They are masters of pathos, those professional train-whistle tuners. They know just what's going to arrow straight through to our hearts. I recall a cowboy movie in which a man was shot near the heart with an arrow that had a detachable head. If he pulled the arrow out, the head would stay in there, and he would surely die. So he had to push the arrow all the way through his chest and out his back, remove the arrowhead, and then draw the unarmed shank back out from the front. He grimaced and trembled, but he lived.

Nothing like that has happened to me. I've just ridden my tricycle, gone to school, greased my bicycle bearings, gotten a job, gotten married, had children, and here I am.

There are lots of stars out tonight—I looked through the glass at one, which broke into two because of a distortion in the glass. Or maybe it was my tears. Nah, just kidding. I'm a child of urban renewal. As I grew up, the elms and the buildings came down. Once my father and I went to the top of Reservoir Hill to walk around the reservoir, which we did every so often. I was six years old. We could see out over the city. He pointed towards downtown. "You see that thing with the three arches?" he said. I said I did. "That's the train station. They're going to tear it down."

I asked him if we could stop them. People were trying, he said, and there was a petition, which was a list of names of people who didn't want it to happen, but it didn't look as if it could be stopped. He and I drove to the train station on a Sunday, a few days after they'd started the demolition. The inside had been covered with tiles. It was now open to the sky; but the fountain was still there by the grand stairway, with a bronze figure of a woman sending forth an eagle. The fountain later disappeared; nobody knows where it is. The building had been built by a local architect named Richard Brinsley, an Arts and Crafts enthusiast, in 1904. There were holes in the side walls where the black ball had smashed, and broken tiles everywhere, but there were many tiles still in good shape, and my father and I filled a wooden crate with them and brought them home. Brinsley had designed the tiles himself—there were four different designs. They were called encaustic tiles. Brinsley also happened to be the architect who had designed our house, which is why my father knew about him—in our attic he found Brinsley's private recipe for stucco: it included horsehair.

Some of the tiles my father gave away to employees, and five he used right away to repair our fireplace, which had been damaged when the couple who owned it before us had ripped out the mantelpiece and installed a narrow strip of moderno-slate, surmounted by an enormous pink mirror. My father took down the mirror and gave it to a man who grew tree peonies, and he chipped out the broken places in the tilework and mixed up some fresh grout and squished the tiles from the train station into place. They fit perfectly—perfectly—as if they were meant to be there. He let me squish one of them in. They had a sort of Celtic design, in green and brown, but with a very soft porous glaze. When it dried, the grout we had used was whiter than the grout that was around the other tiles. It didn't look right, so we touched it up with black Magic Marker. The black, however, was too dark, and then it became my job to Magic Marker all the grout between all the tiles in the fireplace. When I was finished, the fireplace looked deep and rich, with no broken places, and the tiles from the railroad station were like random stars in the sky of the plain brown tiles that had been there. There was no way you could tell that I had used black Magic Marker. My father put a new mantelpiece over the fireplace, an ornate one with two out-scrolling mustaches of dark-stained oak that had been torn out of a church on Main Street and left on the curb, and when it was done, the thing looked as if it had always been there, a fireplace any boy would be proud of.

In place of the Richard Brinsley train station there is now a parking garage where criminals go to hold people up at gunpoint; Amtrak, at great expense, has built a new and pitiful little station nearby that has some blue fiberglass chairs and vending machines in it. The sculpture of the noble-breasted bronze woman and her eagle has never turned up. All that's left of the original station are the tiles in my parents' fireplace—and of course that fireplace isn't my parents' anymore because when they got their divorce, they sold the house. But that's all right—the tiles are permanently fixed in my head; when I look up at night I see them in the constellations, surrounded by black grout.

29

Good morning, it's 6:03 a.m., late. Yesterday I used the toilet plunger on the bathtub drain with great success. The cat was so indignantly hungry this morning that I grabbed a handful of catfood and jingled it into his bowl, and then I brought that hand to my face and smelled it. It smelled quite good—some catfood does. Perhaps my nose is celebrating that it has gotten its land legs back. Cats need to keep the bits of food forever tumbling, half airborne, in their mouths, like clothes in a dryer, or like tiny Hacky Sack balls, and so they're forced to do more head bobbing than seems necessary.

I'm afraid the cat is a compulsive eater. I watched him through the window the other day, after he'd bolted down a full bowl of dry catfood in the shape of little fishes. He was especially displeased with the quality of the snow that cold day—a grimy sort of snow that stuck to his paws, making him shake his hind legs with every step, while he held his head up and looked out for crows and coon cats. Then he stopped and started to retch, his head low, his stomach clenching. Nothing came out, but he had eaten too much too fast. He took a moment to compose himself, and then he went on walking, fluttering his rear paws each time.

This morning I woke up writing an impassioned petition in my head, but impassioned petitions do nothing, and now I'm downstairs. What you don't realize normally, but do just as it begins filling the room through the windows, is how bright but unblinding daylight is. No man-made source can arrive at the particular effortless blueness of this crevice-cleaning light. It is a simple light that goes everywhere but with no heat, aware that it is taken for granted and content to be so.

Very soon, I've got to take a shower and drive Phoebe to school and go to work. It used to be, several long weeks ago, that the shower was the beginning of my day and the place where I did my eyes-closed morning thinking, and I do love the hum of the ceiling fan and the clinking slide of the plastic rings on the shower rod as I pull the curtain closed. I often sing "Eight Days a Week" to the drone of the ceiling fan. And when I reach in (before I get in, so that I won't be blasted with cold or hot) and turn on the control by feel, I can sometimes hear the ringing sound of the water racing up the pipe and smacking against the showerhead, where it is immediately split into two dozen streamlets of fine snickering spray. While it is warming up, I drape my watch over one edge of the sink, and then I wander back into the bedroom to take off my pajamas. I can do this, by the way, without having to bend to the floor to pick them up. Here's how: pin the end of your left pajama leg under your right foot and then lift your left leg, stepping out of the pinned flannel on that side. At this point you've got one pajamaed leg and one naked leg. Then pin the bottom edge of the right pajama leg under your left foot, and bend that knee, drawing off the pajamas entirely—but hold on to the waistband so that instead of their falling to the floor you can ball up the loose and still warm garment and shove it under the pillow for the next night's sleeping.

The showerhead is lower than my head, so I must duck a little, but it's well worth it—those skull-warming drops force out a blubbering sigh of relief. I'm just my shower self—hideous, naked, defenseless. I shave in the shower, eyes closed, mirrorless, checking with my fingertips for places I missed. Of course because I have a beard I have less to shave, but I still have neck and cheeks to do—I balloon out each cheek in turn to make the follicles pop up. Sometimes I fall into the habit of shaving too high on the underside and have to remember to stop earlier on the upstrokes. I don't like beards that fail to cover the corner of the jawbone: that is, beards that are a form of makeup, with sharp cuts and topiary corners. I move the soap, that heavy oval bar, into all the places it needs to go, being sure to rinse it off for the next person—i.e., my wife—after it goes in some of the places. You can make the soap revolve in your hand, like a police car's dome light, just by working your thumb and palm muscles a little: it looks as if the soap is turning of its own accord, and not as if you are turning the soap. Revolving the soap this way several times under the spray is a good way to clean it off. The soap *must* be left clean.

My towel hangs on a rack across the bathroom, too far to reach while standing in the tub after the shower. I don't like leaving puddles on the floor, and I've had little

success when I've tried to shake my legs to get some of
the free water off them before I stepped out. So now I use
my hands as squeegees: starting at midthighs I squeegee
my hands down my legs to my ankles. You would be
surprised at how much water sheets off. In this way I
leave a fairly dry bathroom, even though the drain to the
bathtub is slow enough to count as clogged and, until I
took action yesterday, filled after every shower. The small
fluffy rug next to the shower absorbs the lesser wetness
from my feet.

The reason why the tub was draining so slowly is that
the plumbers installed a kind of drain mechanism whose
metal stopper is unremovable. It can be pulled up about
half an inch and no farther. Once I called the plumber to
see what he could do with this diabolical machine: he
used a bent paper clip to poke in around the drain cap and
withdraw some of the hair-muck, which is just what I
would have done. Paper clips can only do so much, and
yesterday, as I stood in the shower squeegeeing off the
water from my legs, I looked down at my feet, which
were submerged in water that was not trickling out of the
bathtub. There was no sound of draining. The tub drain
was clearly clogged. What could I use to get that clog

moving? Well, why not the toilet plunger? There are two kinds of toilet plunger: the brick-red classic plunger that is able to stand up by itself, and the somewhat newer black rubber plunger, the design of which is more like that of an undersea creature, with a narrowing part meant to go a little ways into the toilet canal, and a higher bell, to thrust out more water and suck in more water with each plunge. These are the double-flush plungers—the kind that we have.

The classic toilet plunger would have been useless on the bathtub, because you couldn't have pushed the bell down, but the black double-flush worked extremely well. I got on my underwear and my shirt and then I pulled back the shower curtain and I put that, of course, none-too-hygienic plunger into the standing water and gave it a lunge, and then another lunge. It made the most wonderful deep squirting noises—huge sucking, bubbling gulps and gasps and noggin-snorts as several pounds of water were thrust down into the drain and forced up in a foul fountain out the overflow valve higher up on the top. I began working with the water, as if I were rocking a car when it's stuck in the driveway, sucking, pushing, sucking, pushing. At one point the drain seemed even worse, and I found that all the turbulence had caused the drain lid to turn and fall shut. When I opened it again and was more careful to center the plunger over the mouth of the drain, I got real results: after one blast, to which I gave the full might of my arms, a supernova of black fragments came up, *God,* and then more with a second plunge, and I knew that without chemicals, without rooting snakes, with only strength and cunning, I had made that water move. I held still for a second to listen: yes, the purling of the water curving away into the pipes. Later there was even a brief vortex, like a rainbow after a storm.

30

Good morning, it's 4:53 a.m.—I brought some wood in from the porch and put it on the fire, and I thought I could make out, in the dimness, a spider or one of those big hopping ants dashing around on the upper surface, trying to escape the heat. But it wasn't a spider or an ant, it was just a bit of black ash being scooted this way and that by the updrafts. Where do the spiders go? One afternoon back in the fall when it was cold but not so cold as it is now, I put a birch log at the top of a fire. The flames lit the white bark, which crackled and curled, and then suddenly a largeish spider climbed into view, making little nervous sprints in one direction and then another. I went into the kitchen and got a small glass. The spider was keeping still by this point—not terribly big, with a dark motif on his yellow abdomen that looked like something you would see on a biker's T-shirt. I put the rim of the glass near him and he sensed the nearby coolness and walked onto it; when I righted the glass he slipped to the bottom. Any time he tried to climb up the edge, as I carried him out the back door, I shook the glass slightly so that he fell back. I poured him out onto the woodpile. He crawled over to the edge of some bark, trying to fit under it, but his abdomen was too big to allow him to pass into the shadows. There was a yellowness to the upper segments of his legs, too. "You have fun," I said to him. It isn't that I think it's horrible to kill a spider, just that there are certain things I would rather not do, and one is to watch a spider catch fire.

It's completely still here. I don't hear a single car. I can see a little indirect glow of the moon on one of the curtains, and when I type my fingers make patterings, like a squirrel spiraling up a tree. The fire today began with the help of a Vermont Trading Company catalog, and I have at the ready the remains of a thick prospectus for a mutual fund, part of which I burned the other day. The prospectus was made of a kind of onionskin—very strong and thin and noisy when turned. You would think it would burn quickly but it is a sluggish starter. Then it flames up just fine.

The spider makes me think of Fidel, my long-ago ant. We got him because my grandmother wanted to get Phoebe a plastic cooking set for her third birthday. At the store, my grandmother brought the cooking set up to the gift-wrap counter, and while it was being wrapped, she went to shop for something else. When she returned, she was given the wrong box, which she mailed to us. And thus Phoebe opened a birthday present that was an ant farm.

But we were all perfectly happy to have an ant farm, and in time we sent away for the ants and poured in the granules and watched them dig their tunnels. They were doing fine in their farm, and then Claire and Phoebe went away for two weeks to visit Claire's parents—this was before Henry was born—and I was left in charge. And it got a lot colder. Some of the ants didn't like the cold and died—when they died they curled up, very conveniently, so that the other ants could carry them to one of two crypts or burial grounds. I kept the ant farm on the mantel, and there wasn't an awful lot I could do about the cold—that house just got cold. After one very cold night there was a widespread curling up and dying of ants. No droplets of springwater or crumbs of saltine would help. But the ants that remained were hardier. They kept digging. There were better tunnels to be made—or not better, just different. One by one they died, until there were two ants left. And then one evening I came home from work and saw that only one ant was now alive. He had buried his friend.

This final ant, however, was a super-ant. He looked the same as the others, but he kept on going. I named him Fidel. I told Claire about Fidel when we talked on the phone—we had no cat or duck back then, so he was my only companion. Fidel kept alive by working, and he was a good example to me. He would hold still for several hours, napping, and then he would begin digging a new tunnel. His tunnel crossed through what had been a grave site, and as he worked his way through, he carried each curled-up ant to a new, better crypt, at a higher elevation, that he made on the right side of the farm, over the plastic barn and silo. After intense struggle, he succeeded in transferring all his fallen comrades from the left-hand crypt to the new right-hand crypt, and he piled the granules of rock or sand over them.

Fidel old boy, Fidel my pal! I kept hearing cavernous choral music when I looked at his purposeful life between those two close-set panes of plastic. I tried to take pictures of him, but the plastic reflected the flash and I got nothing, just a flare of white and an orange date. I would give him a crumb of saltine, and he would spend half an hour burying it. Some of the ants dissolved and became no more than black stains in the sand, and yet Fidel lived on, slower but still active. He wasn't sentimental: I watched him uncover a bit of one of his associates—a leg—which he unceremoniously kicked behind him.

My family returned, and I was no longer alone. But lonely Fidel lived on for two more weeks, then three, a month, *more than a month*—he lived longer alone than he had lived with company. I ran out of springwater and used tap water, and he seemed not to mind. He thrived on tap water, in fact—maybe it was the secret elixir of longevity for him. He knew that nobody was alive to carry his curled-up body to a resting place, so he didn't die. To him devolved the full responsibility of the farm. He moved his feelers in little circles—he felt everything before he lifted it. Sometimes he worried me because he rested by tucking his abdomen up under himself, and I thought maybe he was winding down, but no—I dripped in a little water, and his feelers began going, and he went into a rain-avoidance routine, hurrying down to a dry tunnel. Or I would breathe on the plastic where he was, and he would sense the warmth and move an antenna, then turn and cling to the fogged-over part of the plastic.

"Is the ant still alive?" Phoebe asked one day. She was wearing two aprons over her dress and a pink blanket over her head, surmounted by a fez hat. I said yes, he was still alive. She said she was sorry that the other ants had died. "When we first got them, they were nice little ants."

For two days I forgot about Fidel, and then, in the middle of the night, I remembered him. I shined a flashlight on him, sure that I would find that he was no more. He looked dusty. I dripped in some water and a cracker crumb—an earlier crumb had a fine haze of mold on it—and spoke encouragingly to him. And he moved. I was interested by the ends of his legs, which I thought must be wearing away with all that scrambling over sand boulders. He had learned to brace himself against the plastic as he maneuvered an ant body up an incline. Moving ant bodies had become his whole life.

And finally he did die, as every ant will. I kept his

farm, however, the legacy of tunnels and graveyards that he had completely rebuilt after he had become the sole representative of his civilization. For two years it stood on a table in my office. When we moved, I packed it in a box, wrapped carefully in white packers' paper. But I wasn't too surprised when I unpacked it and saw that all the tunnels were gone—the ant farm was now just loose sand with some dirt specks in it.

31

Good morning, it's 5:25 a.m., boys and girls. I seem to be down to a few matches skidding around in the little red box. I struck one of the remaining ones and it broke. As a result of the breakage, the match head must have been nearer to my nose than it normally is, so that when the first flare flowed out, going sideways as it does before the teardrop shape can form, I received a sudden sharp smell in my nostril that sent my head back, the smell of a new flame. It was as sharp as when some carbon dioxide from a gulp of root beer accidentally backs up into your sinus and your head rocks. I lit the under-fire and then laid the spent and broken match on top of two quarter-logs—sometimes a little piece of something on top of the fire seems to work like a fishing lure, drawing the goldfish flame upward through the cracks and around the corners, where the splinters turn black and crumple, glowing.

At twilight yesterday Henry and I went on a walk in the woods, where there were tracks of rabbit and deer, and the feetmarks of some small birds. When it got too dark, we came back to the barn and dug another tunnel in the plow pile. Because there have been so many thaws and refreezings, the snow in the pile has a granular consistency for several feet, and then finally you find the virginal substance underneath: bluish white and freshly fluffy even after all these weeks. Then a heat-seeking wind came up, and it filched all the heat from under my arms and around my ribs. But when we went in, the duck stood by the back door quacking actively for warm water with food pellets sprinkled in it. I carried her to her duckhouse and got her settled, and draped the blanket over the roof, stuffing a fold of it into the crack between the roof and the sides so that her night would be a little warmer.

I want to take care of the world. Sometimes I think of a helmet with a set of plastic earflaps that I swivel down over my ears. There are holes on the outside of the earflaps that pick up sounds of distress from far away. It is like listening to the whales groan and squeal—there is

usually one cry that is prominent, and, by turning my
head from side to side, I use the signals reaching each ear
to guide me to where the crime or misery is. I can fly, of
course.

Meanwhile, Jumbo California Navel Oranges are
selling two for seventy-nine cents, according to the
supermarket circular I just crumpled and stuffed into a
fire hole—which doesn't seem all that cheap. Last night,
Claire and I watched a cable-TV biography of James
Taylor—what a voice that man has—and we paid the
bills, and now there's the slush pile of torn envelopes and
little cross-advertisements that come in with them; the
watches and the luggage sets and the insurance plans that
add a few dollars a month. I'm burning some of the
envelopes that Christmas cards came in—not the cards.
Envelopes burn well, because the torn places catch
quickly. Claire started paying most of the bills two years
ago, after we got one too many of those polite
reminders—"All of Us Forget on Occasion"—which
would shade into "Your Account Is Seriously Past Due."
Bills are just little wrapped enclosures. If you don't open
them you don't know whether they're angry or not. The
credit-card companies love me, in truth, because I'm

always good for a late fee and a superhigh interest rate, and yet I'm not going to default on them. And yet once I do open the envelopes and I start paying, I enjoy it, and I still pay some of the charge accounts that have work expenses on them. Also I put on the stamps. I suppose common practices will change soon and become electronic, just as now we're no longer sent our canceled checks but rather little scanned pictures of our checks. But what a pleasure it is to have winnowed out all the glossy enclosures and have gotten things down to the essentials: the payment stub, torn off, and the handwritten check, and the return envelope, and the stamp. Then you straighten up that little stack of paid bills, all in envelopes that are slightly dissimilar sizes, and see the addresses peeping through the windows, and you feel good. Some billers, like the bank that holds the mortgage, don't believe in sending return envelopes, and we have to supply a new one of our own.

A succession of days is like a box of new envelopes. Each envelope is flimsy and can be treated as two-dimensional. But when you pull out all the envelopes from the box at once, there is a hard place in the middle—a thick lump—that you wouldn't expect

envelopes to have. The lump is created by the intersection
of the four triangles in the middle of the back. Most of
the envelope has only two layers of paper, but on the
place where you lick the flap there are three: the front,
the lower edge, and the gummed edge. And in the middle
of the back there is a place, sometimes two places, of
further overlap, and it feels as if the envelopes must be
holding something quite hard, or sharp, even—but of
course they're empty. You notice it when you are writing
thank-yous for wedding presents, or when you are
sending out Christmas cards, or if you have bought a new
box of envelopes and you see the edges of them through
the clear window and you want to compress them, since
envelopes are so springily compressible—and as you
reach around them and squeeze them you feel the nugget,
the something that isn't in the envelopes but is of the
envelopes. I would almost say that there is a hint on the
meaning of life there, in that revealed kernel. That's what
they feel like, in fact, these hard places—little popcorn
kernels or apple seeds.

32

Good morning, it's 5:15 a.m.——While I was building the fire I noticed a warm glow coming in one of the windows. I thought there must be a light on in some other part of the house, but the angle was wrong. I went to the window and saw that the inside lights of the minivan were on. They looked quite cozy. I didn't want to have a dead battery two hours from now, so I found my coat in the dark, slipped on a pair of cold boots that were on the porch, and crunched outside.

It was dark and starry and the wind was up. I was shocked by how cold it was. I haven't been outside in the middle of winter at four-thirty in the morning——except perhaps to hop into a cab to go to an airport——ever, I don't think. I opened and then closed the rear door of the car—one inside light turned off right away, and then the dome light in the front did the slow fade-out that automotive engineers believe is an improvement. Good. Just to be sure the battery was all right, I reached in and turned on the ignition: the radio came on, loudly playing Brahms. I withdrew the key and was done with the car. But I stood for a moment to sense the cold's spaciousness and impersonality. It was remarkable to think that human beings felt that they could endure in this dark, inhospitable place. If I slipped and fell and was unable to move I'd die. And yet the duck, more or less immobile under her shroud, lived through the night just fine, and was ready to burble in the warm water of her eating bowl as soon as I came out. I heard the wind in the denuded trees—there was no upper hissing of leaf wind, just the longer wailing whistles that the old branches make.

When I turned toward the house, I saw another glow in a living-room window. I crunched through the snow up the little rise and peered into the living room. "Will you look at that," I said. There was my fire, as orange as could be, looking warm. I half expected to see myself sitting there, in my bathrobe, but the chair was empty.

Now I'm back inside. I leaned forward just now so that I could turn to the right and take hold of the handle of my coffee mug, and I moved it around towards me in a wide slow curve, and the sight of this movement in the fiery dimness had a beauty to it. Why are things beautiful? I don't know. That's a good question. Isn't it pleasing when you ask a question of a person, a teacher, or a speaker, and he or she says, That's a good question? Don't you feel good when that happens? Sometimes when the fire puffs out it gets so black it's almost frightening. I don't want to use the last match. Finally a crumple will catch and burn down to fireworms. Then darkness again, and cold. That's what I like about this living room: when I come down here, it is really cold. The chair is cold to the touch when I sit down on it. When I sit here and breathe in and out with my eyes closed I can think of myself as a spinning tire, rocking back and forth past a low point in the frozen driveway. The tire wants to spin its own grave, melting the ice to its shape, and you have to help it get beyond that wish. You drive as high up on the upslope as you can and then, just when the car is weightless, you clunk the transmission into reverse and use the ride back down into the self-created valley to help you over it, and if you don't make it the first time, rock again. As you move the shifter back and forth, from reverse to drive to reverse to drive, and you begin to smell that faint whiff of hot rubber, you feel the same sort of wild joy you felt when you first learned how to swing, and learned how to go higher without being pushed. Actually it's better than swinging on a swing, since with a swing you can never quite go so high that the swing will fly all the way around, but when you're stuck in the driveway you finally reach the point where you are no longer tethered to a particular harmonic center point, and you churn off on your errand, sometimes at a slight diagonal, as one wheel pushes better than the other.

33

Good morning, it's 4:49 a.m., and this is my last match. After I lit a few corners of paper and cardboard, I let the match fall onto a fold of a Circuit City flyer where I'm sure it will contribute its pittance.

What's the best thing I can think of at this very second? Best thing. Let's think. All right. Okay, one time Claire and I were driving to the beach and Claire pointed out a Yield sign standing by a field. "Mist," she said. The early sun was heating up the reflective substance on one side of the sign and evaporating the dew or night-rain that was clinging to it. Morning mist rising from the Yield sign against a field: that's one thing. Here's another. Claire and I were sitting on the couch. This was seven years ago. I was doing some work, she was reading a paperback and giving our infant son milk from her breast. "I've got a new way to turn the page," she said. I looked over. One of her arms was holding up Henry and so was out of commission. The other was holding the paperback splayed open. When it was time, she put the tip of her tongue on the lower right-hand corner of the right-hand page. The tip held the paper, and by moving her head to the left, she could make the page slide and buckle, whereupon her thumb dove underneath it and was able to send it over to the little finger on the far side. So, Claire turning the pages with her tongue: that's another thing.

You know what I think I'll do? I think I'll creep back in bed, very carefully so as not to joggle too much, pull the covers over me, relax all my muscles, and go back to sleep for a little while next to her, then get up at a normal time.

I tossed my apple core into the fire, and then, as an afterthought, I crunched the empty matchbox into a mound of orange bits the size of sugar cubes that had fallen away from a log. It caught right away and burned with a generous yellow flame. In thirty seconds it had curled away into a twist of ash and the fire was orange again. I was done.